Tamarisk

I sold military books for more than two decades, and I read many. This gripping novel slow-burns its way into your heart. Angela Locke understands the difference between *how* people endure and *why*. Fear haunts the told; regret, the telling. Not only fiction, but a hundred realities are being retold. You will dread the ending, but like them, you will go on.
Brindley Hallam Dennis, author of *A Penny Spitfire*

Tamarisk is magnificent. Gripping and beautifully written by an author who has a deep understanding of France and the Roma people. It comes from the heart but is deeply and lovingly researched. Suspenseful, compassionate and full of hope, and also moving and wise: The perfect novel for our difficult times.
Grevel Lindop, former professor of English, Manchester University, and author of *Travels on the Dance Floor*, *A Literary Guide to the Lake District*, *Charles Williams: The Third Inkling*, and others

Angela Locke's latest novel is dramatic and vivid, a story of loss and regrowth set in a Europe recovering from the destruction of the Second World War. Through the strength of their love for each other and for their daughter, Marie, and for Aishe, a Roma girl whom they have adopted, Pierre and Rebecca recreate a life of hope for a new future. Pierre rebuilds the ruined farmhouse in Normandy where, on Special Operations behind enemy lines, he fell in love with Rebecca. *Tamarisk* has an authenticity that comes from many years of detailed research, from a close acquaintance with the Normandy countryside and from an emotional sympathy with the times. The years after the War were years of stress and dislocation. This remarkable story, symbolised by the miraculous recovery of the tamarisk tree, shows how one family found renewed hope after the traumas they had faced in the brutality and inhumanity of that most terrible of all wars.

Steve Matthews, bookseller, bookshop owner, publisher, author, reviewer, and historian

You might want to fasten your seat belt as you're drawn into Pierre's story from the moment his parachute opens until the very last page of Angela Locke's *Tamarisk*. Her characters are so finely drawn, so real, that they will stay with the reader for a very long time. She has masterfully created a world that takes us into the lives of displaced persons in every walk of life, including the Romany people, whose stories were woefully unknown to us, and the beyond-brave people of the French Resistance. In this novel, we run the gamut of kindnesses toward strangers to the unspeakable horrors we humans can inflict upon each other. It's a story of survival — even for the most vulnerable of us. Angela skillfully unfolds and intertwines the stories of seemingly disparate people.

Tamarisk is, sadly, a timely piece, even though it is set during and post-World War II. Angela has created a world of hope and resilience despite all odds. She reminds us that the human spirit is a beautiful thing to behold. It is her gift to us. A gift that continues to give, even after we close the book.

Rebekah Spivey, USA, author of *Marigolds in Boxes*, *Flight Plan*, and *Rugburns*; editor, writing coach, and a certified facilitator for Women Writing for Change

Angela Locke takes us back in time, through one of the greatest tragedies history has ever seen, and leads her characters, and the reader, gently to safe ground. Rural France is so beautifully evoked, 'Le Tamaris' a haven of peace and healing.

Kathleen Jones, author and poet, Royal Literary Fellow

Tamarisk

Love and War in France
A Novel

Tamarisk

Love and War in France
A Novel

Angela Locke

**TOP HAT
BOOKS**

Winchester, UK
Washington, USA

JOHN HUNT PUBLISHING

First published by Top Hat Books, 2024
Top Hat Books is an imprint of John Hunt Publishing Ltd., No. 3 East St., Alresford,
Hampshire SO24 9EE, UK
office@jhpbooks.com
www.johnhuntpublishing.com
www.tophat-books.com

For distributor details and how to order please visit the 'Ordering' section on our website.

Text copyright: Angela Locke 2023

ISBN: 978 1 80341 486 7
978 1 80341 487 4 (ebook)
Library of Congress Control Number: 2023909351

Design: Lapiz Digital Serivices

UK: Printed and bound by CPI Group (UK) Ltd, Croydon, CR0 4YY
US: Printed and bound by Thomson-Shore, 7300 West Joy Road, Dexter, MI 48130

Previously Published by Angela Locke

Mr Mullett Owns A Cloud
Chatto & Windus
ISBN 10: 0952574292
ISBN 13: 9780952574293

Search Dog
Souvenir Press Ltd
ISBN 10: 0285628143
ISBN 13: 9780285628144
ISBN 10: 0747401497
ISBN 13: 9780747401490

Sam & Co
Souvenir Press Ltd
ISBN 10: 0285629360
ISBN 13: 9780285629363

Hearing Dog, with Jenny Harmer
Souvenir Press Ltd
ISBN 10: 0285634003
ISBN 13: 9780285634008

Dreams of the Blue Poppy
Robert Hale Ltd
ISBN 10: 0709082827
ISBN 13: 9780709082828

On Juniper Mountain
O-Books
ISBN 10: 1846943019
ISBN 13: 9781846943010
ISBN 13: 978178099605

Mrs Mullett and the Cloak of Gaia
Bookcase
ISBN 13: 9781912181056

Poetry:

North Face
Pleiades Press
ISBN 10: 0951438808
ISBN 13: 9780951438800

Into the Lotus
Pleiades Press and Nepal

Sacred Earth
Pleiades Press

Walls at the World's End
Senhouse Roman Army Museum

Whale Language: Songs of Iona
Indigo Dreams
ISBN 10: 1907401504
ISBN 13: 9781907401503

About the Author

Angela Locke is an award-winning journalist, author and poet. She has six fiction and non-fiction books published, widely translated and serialised, four poetry collections and the film script *In the Mind of Man*. Her first book was *Mr Mullett Owns a Cloud* (Chatto & Windus). Her novel *Dreams of the Blue Poppy* (Robert Hale and ebook) is set in Cumbria and the Himalayas, and her travel book *On Juniper Mountain* (O-Books and ebook) is about her journey in Nepal. She holds an MA in Creative Writing and leads International Creative Writing Retreats on Iona, in the English Lake District and France. Angela is Writer-in-Residence at Senhouse Roman Museum in Maryport, where she runs an annual Literature Festival. She is President of The Juniper Trust (thejunipertrust.org), a charity working in education and health across the developing world. Angela spends as much time as she can in France, where she used to have a house in Normandy, and where *Tamarisk* is set.

More detail on her website at angelalocke.co.uk

SOLDATS SANS UNIFORME
POUR HONNEUR ET LA LIBERTÉ
ILS ONT FAIT LE SACRIFICE DE LEUR VIE

Memorial beside the N.23 North of Angers
to reseau Hercule/Buckmaster
and reseau Pascal/Sacristain/Buckmaster:
sixty-five lives lost

This book is dedicated to the memory of all those who lost their lives in the concentration camps, including more than one million Roma people wiped out by Hitler's Nazis. Apart from major historical figures, all characters, and the *reseaux* to which they belonged, although inspired by real events, are entirely fictional or fictionalised. Many place names have been changed.

Preface

I would like to thank the staff of the Imperial War Museum, who gave me generous and invaluable help in my research from the 1980s onwards, and special clearance for access to classified documents relating to SOE, and the experiences of agents in France. I am also indebted to the late Major Gordon Staniforth of the Worcestershire Regiment, who parachuted into Normandy with the advance forces on D-Day 21, who gave me inestimable support and advice in the writing of this book.

I have been honoured to hear and read many testaments of the work of SOE agents in France. I am deeply indebted to their generosity in sharing their stories.

We were privileged to be in Normandy for the 50th Anniversary of the Liberation. I will never forget being embraced by an elderly lady in tears outside the *pharmacie*, who wanted to thank us, as representatives of the Allied forces, for freeing them from Nazi oppression. Here, in Avranches, General Patten's tank stands as a monument on the roundabout at the top of the town, surrounded by flowers. It is we too who should thank the French people, as well as all other peoples who suffered under the yoke of Occupation, for their stoicism and bravery.

Grateful thanks are more than due for her dedicated help to my wonderful secretary, Clare Morton, in the preparation of the manuscript, and to Diane Scott for her help with earlier versions. Also to managing editor Frank Smecker for all his unfailing help and support with *Tamarisk*.

1

What would it be like? Not like coming home, wherever home was. Pierre sat in the green dark, the plane's engines vibrating through him. Out there somewhere was his grandmother's house by the sea. She was dead now. Somewhere too in France his English father was buried, on another battlefield.

The dispatcher opened a trap door in the floor, and the night came flooding in. Below, a broad river like a silver nail file in the moon, trees running, wooden cows, bridges flashing like piano keys.

A red light. Dispatcher's arm up, green lamp. A jerk as the static lines did their stuff. The parachute, a mushroom swaying him down.

France, his mother country, below him in the mist.

Three bars of light shone upward as the world rushed to meet him. He hit hard. Winded, he lay on his back, struggling with his harness.

All around him were figures, waist-deep in the white mist. Canisters thudded down around him.

'I say! Can't someone give me a hand?'

A light shone full in his face, and he was pulled to his feet, still trussed up like a chicken. Two shapes stripped him of his parachute and flying suit. Further away, other figures were working waist high in mist, silent as ghosts, disentangling canisters. Then quiet, mist curling in eddies where the men had been.

One of the shadows sidled up to him, cigarette stub glowing.

'Is that you, Maurice?'

'Yes!'

'Come with us now!'

The man took the cigarette stub out of his mouth, pinched the end and put it back in his pocket.

'Camel dung,' he whispered. 'Pure shit. Hope you brought some decent cigarettes.'

He wondered whether they should be moving out of the landing field. It seemed dangerous just to be standing there.

'It's OK now! The cart has come back.'

Three more shadows detached themselves from the trees.

'Sink this lot! Get a move on!'

The bundle of parachute, flying suit and helmet was handed over.

'And if you pinch the silk again for your wife's panties, I'll skin you alive. It's got to be buried. Understand!'

'Fuck you.'

They came out of the field through a gap in the hedge. Pierre looked back for a second. Nothing. A field sleeping under the moon. No longer even the drone of a distant aircraft.

They loaded him up into the cart and covered him with straw. They lurched along the track. He felt the hard boards against his hip. He rehearsed it in his mind. He was Jean Vacher, SOE code name 'Maurice', small-time fisherman off the Banks, small-time farmer, ex-Boules Champion. His hair had been cut in England by a barber from Brest who had left France in 1939, his suit made for him by an ex-patriot tailor. In another life.

The cart stopped. Muttered voices, a low laugh. Then a couple of outraged screams which made his blood freeze. A large object plummeted down in the straw beside him. A strong smell of pig. He rolled over hastily to the far side of the cart.

Hands rearranged the straw.

I am Jean Vacher. My parents are dead. Killed in the bombings. I never married.

Greasy black peaked cap and fisherman's smock packed away in a battered case with his razor, and spare underpants darned with French cotton. The FANY officer had planted the stub of a cigarette (one never threw away a cigarette stub in wartime France), a used, screwed-up bus ticket to Rouen, an almost empty packet of Gauloises, a French button, a length of ersatz string smelling of fish, the stub of a French pencil and a battered holy picture of Our Lady with the faded inscription 'À Jean, Juillet 1932'. In this other life, he had been confirmed in July, when he was twelve, in the church of St Armand, close to Dieppe.

Some small change and a money belt containing 500,000 francs which he would have to get rid of quickly. Identity card, ration card and all the other papers he would need.

It had been a fine day in early September. Stubble was still standing in the fields. Only land girls and old men left for the harvest. He had been driven to the airfield by a FANY officer. She had stopped to move a hedgehog out of the road, curled in a tight ball. He remembered how hedgehog tasted, baked in the fire.

Back in France, someone was whispering close to his ear. 'Josephine is very ferocious! Watch your bollocks.'

The cart resumed its hypnotic swaying. A loud challenge shattered the calm. He felt the cart pull to a halt.

'Yes, Monsieur! I know it is some time after curfew. But that vicious bloody sow wandered off into the forest. We have had a devil of a job to catch her.'

Footsteps beside the cart. Pierre poked Josephine sharply in the ribs. She shot out of sleep with an indignant scream, trampling his thigh.

'You see, Monsieur! She is truly vicious. Last week she bit the mayor — a chunk like so. Can you wonder we had such trouble?'

'Hurry up!'

Josephine spat and screamed, one trotter still planted in Pierre's thigh.

'Don't let it happen again. This curfew is for your protection. Don't forget.'

The cart moved off slowly, the driver whistling into the dark. Tree shadows flicked across the straw. Pierre heard a train, rattling through the steel-trapped night; the German night. There was a change of rhythm as the cart swung left. Cobbles clacked against wheels. They stopped, and hands grabbed him. The moon came out from behind a cloud and lit up the tops of a house, chimneys stark against the sky. A door opened, and he pushed into a brightly lit room, thick with cigarette smoke. A smell of cooking.

'Here you are, Madame LeFaivre! Maurice has arrived! Now's your chance to get inside the trousers of a British agent!'

'A bit more respect if you don't mind, or I'll knock your block off.'

'The pig got him. Just there.'

Someone grabbed his thigh.

'Look at that! His trousers all torn. It's a disgrace. She's a cow, that pig. The sooner she gets made into chitterlings the better.'

'You liar. She's the love of your life. You'd sooner get rid of the missus.'

'I can manage, thank you. I don't need attention.'

'Come on, mate. We're only joshing. Get your trousers down. We're all friends here.'

'Shut up! Just look at the poor lad. Blood on his trousers and he's covered in mud. Claude! You and your black market pig. You'll get us all shot. And for what — just to spite the Boches! Is it worth it?'

'It's for profit, Madame, not just for spite! Profit, Madame! A serious business.'

'Monsieur, please come into the back kitchen and I'll fix that cut. And you lot can shut up!'

Mme LeFaivre brought a bowl of water and dabbed his thigh, looking up at him.

'They'll take you over to Rebecca's, to *Le Tamaris*, as soon as we can. It's a lot safer. No one ever goes out to that place. It's overgrown since the old man took bad. He's blind too. She does what she can, but they need another pair of hands.'

'I won't be able to be much help. I'm going to be busy.'

'Yes, yes. I know. I'm just saying. Here! Take these old trousers. I'll get these ones washed and mended tonight. There's a lot of blood. Just look at that! She really had a go at you. Not much of a welcome! I'll put them over the stove. They'll be dry in the morning.'

'Is Rebecca's house really OK?'

'Oh yes. She wouldn't let anything past her. She's a fierce one. Mind you, if it weren't for the old man, she'd be off like a shot. Wants to go to England to train as a radio operator. You can understand it. Not much for a young girl here, and the old man isn't easy.'

'So it's safe?'

'Oh yes. You'll be alright there for a while. But nothing's safe for ever. You know how it is. Father sent Paul over to tell her. I hope he got through. He'll give her all the details. Well, what we knew, anyway. She'll be expecting you. She's a good lass.'

'Thank you!'

Mme LeFaivre put her hands on her knees and straightened up.

'It's nothing. At least it looks more respectable. And you couldn't go around with blood on your trousers. Now, why don't you come back in and have something to eat? They're not a bad bunch. They'll do anything for you. Once they know you're OK. You just have to take a bit of stick. You know how it is. A family, that's what it's like. Like coming home.'

He went back into the room. They introduced themselves. Claude Durand, dark and thin. Genier hugely fat, spilling over two chairs; a pinstripe suit, shoes down-at-heel. LeFaivre, the old farmer, and his wife. Young Jean-Marc, the communist, who had been at the Sorbonne before the war, now in hiding from the STO — *Service Travail Obligatoire* — which took the young men away to labour camps. Jean-Marc would go to the *maquis* in the hills, if he could. Robert, the policeman, was sitting with a girl, Madeleine, holding hands.

He could not yet see that, with his weapons, his briefings, his plans for the *reseau*, for many of them he was to be their executioner. If, that night, he could have understood, it would have been harder to begin.

2

Paul burst into the kitchen. He had ridden fast, cross-country.

'They want you to hide him!' He was out of breath.

Rebecca crossed to the sink, and filled a cup with water.

'Here! Take this.'

'Thanks! I would have got here yesterday but there were road blocks at Sainte Croix. He's landed already. In a field not far from the LeFaivre's farm. Jean Vacher, that's his name. Code name Maurice. Supposed to be a fisherman, some relative of yours. Coming to help you, because your grandfather's blind. That's his cover.'

He took a gulp of water. 'Are you still OK to do it?'

'Of course. It'll be exciting!' She looked across at Papi. The old man seemed to be asleep.

'You're off the beaten track. It won't be for long. There was to be a drop of weapons and supplies too. Cigarettes, guns, plastic explosive, the usual. We'll be the best equipped group in France!'

'We'll keep him safe. Don't worry!'

'You'll have to watch he doesn't get taken by the STO. Anyway, he will have spent at least one night at the LeFaivre farm, so they can brief him.'

'When will he get here? I need to get the room ready. And we'll have to get some food in.'

'Maybe he'll be here today. Anyway, don't worry about that. Just be ready. Mme LeFaivre sent food — in my pannier. Smoked bacon.'

The old man opened his eyes. 'We don't need no help! We killed a pig last back end.'

'We're very grateful,' she said. 'Please thank her when you see her.'

'I've never seen a British agent,' Paul said. 'I reckon he'll be quite old. Most of them have been in the first war. A bit past it, probably.'

'It would be nice if he was young,' Rebecca thought. 'Someone to talk to. But it was still exciting. A British agent in the house! He might get me to England. I could start training as a radio operator. I know I could do it!'

It might be a way out. Some days she could scream. That winch cutting her hands in the frost, having to be nice to the Boches just to get out and fish in the bay. But how could she leave Papi? He depended on her. After all, he had taken her in when her parents were killed.

'That's fixed then. They'll be grateful. He can't hang around so near to Sainte Croix. It's too risky.'

She got up from the table. 'Don't worry. We'll take care of him. I'll explain to Papi. He's English, after all, though no one remembers that. He hates the Boches as much as we do.'

She knew she had a level head. Chatting up the German sentry on the beach, though it made her want to throw up. Remembering his bombs had dropped on her parents when they were working at the hospital in Evreux.

When Paul left, Papi opened his eyes again.

'When's he coming, then? The British agent?' No flies on him.

3

'We're sending you to *Le Tamaris* first light tomorrow. It's only ten miles the other side of Sainte Croix, nearer to Château-Le-Vigny.' Robert stubbed out his cigarette on his shoe and carefully pinched the end. 'It's good to smoke a whole one for a change. Anyway, we'll keep in touch. It won't be too difficult to send a courier up there.'

Pierre leaned across the Michelin map and traced with his forefinger.

'Where is it? And how long will it be safe?'

'It's here. Beyond the crossroads. OK enough for a bit, we hope. The girl is keen to help. She's been nagging on about joining.'

'Yes, you'll be safe enough there. No one ever goes out to the farm. And the old man will be glad to help the British.'

He stood up and removed his cap, rubbing a grubby forefinger across the scarlet line his cap had left behind.

'We have friends in the *mairie*. We've got the papers here.'

'Thank you. You've taken a lot of risks.'

'It was really Robert who took the risks. He's the policeman! He got you a permit to enter the *Zone Interdit*. You have to cross it for a short while. Here!'

LeFaivre circled the map with his pencil.

'The Zone's tricky?'

'Tricky, but not impossible. If you have the right papers, it's easy enough. See, here it's twenty-five-kilometres deep, and you must just cross a corner. The farm's close to the sea. It's such a small road — you would be very unlucky to be stopped. There's some important information you can gather along the coast. The German Wall, they say, will stretch from the North Cape right round to the south of Brest. It's to keep the Anglo-Saxons out!'

'How do you know all this?'

He grinned. 'Don't ask! It happens there's an old Feldwebel of the Wehrmacht staying with Michel Dayne up at *Grande Colline*. They have had some good chats around the fire. A glass or two of Calvados works miracles. You've just got today to memorise the map. It's our only one and we can't give it to you.'

Robert came into the yard, wheeling an ancient bicycle.

'Look after it! We haven't got many left. And good luck!'

Early next morning Madame LeFaivre handed Pierre a parcel.

'A little salt pork and bread. You'll have a good table at *Le Tamaris*. The old man likes his food. But it's a few miles, and you may be hungry. If you ask me, and I'll be told off saying it, you look too young to be doing such a job. Young enough to be my son. He's been taken for the STO. I don't know if I'll ever see him again.'

She dabbed her eyes with her apron. 'We're old and we don't have any expectations. Not after this war. But you — you have your whole life ahead of you. If you were my son, I'd keep you safe. I wish I'd never let François go. I should have hidden him, sent him to the *maquis*! But we didn't understand anything then.'

'Leave him alone, Mother.' LeFaivre stood in the doorway. 'He knows what he's doing. They wouldn't send him otherwise.'

'I'm fine,' he said. 'Don't worry about me.'

'All the same...' She leaned forward and kissed him on the cheek. 'There were roadblocks outside Ste Acquire yesterday, but they've gone now. Anyway, keep to the back roads while you can. You need to get there before the curfew. You'll be alright at the farm, but you'll have to watch that Rebecca. She'll be nagging you every day about getting to England. Wants to train as a wireless operator, she says. She's hot-headed enough to do it.'

'Can we trust her?'

'She was a real handful when she arrived — after her parents were killed. But she's tough. She's had to cope with a lot. Then her grandmother died last year. And the old man is blind. She runs that farm by herself — what's left of it. It isn't easy for her, but she's a good lass underneath.'

She stood and watched as he cycled out of the farmyard, a small figure tossing grain from her apron pocket to the hens around her feet.

As he passed through Sainte Croix, the long, cobbled hill and across the square, the first few housewives were coming down for their baguettes, oilcloth bags on their arms. There were dogs asleep in doorways of shuttered houses. He didn't see the first German truck until he was urging the ancient, iron-frame bicycle up the hill, between the villas on the far side of the town. It came roaring past and he overbalanced into the ditch. An old woman was washing the pavement. She leant on her broom and watched him clamber out and straighten the wheel of his bicycle. There was a smell of dust, cats and old drains. Even here, in the prosperous district, it was the smell of war and hopelessness.

4

After the town, he stopped on an empty stretch of road. He would be close to the Forbidden Zone for a few kilometres, as the lane bent towards the sea. There was a fresh morning wind now, sharp with autumn. He could smell the sea and there was that wide blankness of sky. The lane was empty, slippery with yellow leaves. The Zone was very narrow here, because of the long inlet which indented the coast.

As he rounded a corner, he found himself on the cliffs. It was high tide below. A broad stream fanned down and spread across the sand. The wind was blowing. Far out on the misty water a fishing boat lazed across the sea.

He looked down. Some fifty yards below him, embedded in the cliff, was a gun emplacement with its gun cocked, an obscene phallus rearing over the beach. Barbed wire, tangled with feathers of birds and strangled bladder wrack. There would be death's head mines below the sand.

The head of a German soldier appeared, framed by the tamarisk which grew on the cliffs. Just like home in Brittany, he thought. So long ago. The soldier was looking out to sea. He crouched down, trying to breathe quietly, smelling that truffle smell of France. Those scents again, the scents of his childhood, damp earth and leaf.

That was a stupid thing to do, he thought. He came to a small junction to the right, hardly more than a path, and a small green and white sign — *La Ferme*. It had to be here. He visualised the map in his mind, and turned off up the track. Bushes and small trees of feathery tamarisk were rooted in the salty soil on the sandy path. It was still close to the sea. He ran his bicycle into a tangle of briar and left it, picking his way forward.

The tunnel of undergrowth opened up. There was a track and the courtyard of a farm. He went on cautiously, lifting the last fronds of tamarisk aside. Unexpectedly, the ground slipped away from beneath his feet, and he was on the edge of a large pond. A frantic squawking as ducks and geese legged it out of the shallows into the safety of the yard.

Then he saw the girl. She was standing on the far side of the pond, clogs firmly planted in the mud, scrubbing brush in one hand, a milk churn in the other. Her hair was very red, down to her waist.

He skirted the edge of the pond. The girl saw him and turned away, working the pump. Water gushed over the side of the churn. She dropped the handle and began to scrub, tossing her hair out of her eyes.

He walked up to her, skidding a little in the mud. She stopped scrubbing and turned a white face to him.

'Monsieur?'

'I have good prawns to sell. Will you buy some?'

'No, we already bought prawns from Monsieur Guillard.'

He waited.

'So?' A pause.

'I'm Maurice,' he said.

'Now I'm confused! They told us your name would be Jean Vacher. You're Grandfather's nephew!'

'Maurice is my operational name. I keep it all the time. The other names are just for cover. I change them when I have to.'

'I see. I think. So what *is* your name?'

'Jean would be better for now.'

She looked at him, tossing her hair back with that long shake. She had very brown eyes, and freckles.

'You don't...' she hesitated, '...you don't seem old enough to be Grandfather's nephew.' She was looking at him seriously. 'He's a very old man. Couldn't you be his grand-nephew? That would be better.'

15

She leaned down again to the pump, the water leaping out of the old green pipe, splintering on the side of the silver churn. The ducks waddled slowly back to the pond, exhibiting effrontery with every step.

'You see, the ducks aren't used to people using the old track.'

'The old track?'

She stood up and lifted the churn over the pump.

'Visitors usually come by the front entrance. It's much grander.' She lifted her chin towards the wide gateway between two ancient griffons, where the road swept muddily out of the farm. She turned her back, carrying the churn in a swinging movement across the yard.

'I'm Rebecca,' she shouted over her shoulder. 'I arrange everything. Come on.

Grandfather's been waiting.'

She dropped the milk churn with others by the door of the barn. He followed her into the house. It was very dark after the sun, huge and high, and her feet in the clogs clattered on the hollowed flagstones. A range stretched almost to the ceiling beside an empty fireplace; there were two wooden chairs and a long table. An old man sat with his back to the light, mending a net which sprawled around his feet.

He lifted his head, and Rebecca knelt in front of him, her hands resting on his.

'He's here,' she said.

'Ah! The British agent!' the old man nodded.

'We have to call him Jean, Papi.' She looked across at Pierre, a measuring look. 'And remember we mustn't tell anyone why he's here. The Germans will come if we do! Do you understand?'

He nodded slowly, with blind, blank eyes.

Squatting, Pierre took Papi's light, dry hand.

'Pleased to meet you, sir.'

'You must be hungry.' Rebecca said. 'I'll make us something.'

'I've got those prawns in my saddlebag. They're fresh. Not just for cover!'

'We can have those with soup. I made some yesterday.'

'Have you always been here, in this house?'

'It's a long story. My parents were killed early in the war. Then the nuns looked after me for a while. They were very good to me. Anyway, in the end they found a way to send me here. Grandmother was alive then. She died last year. It killed her too, this shitty war. And Papi has always been blind, since I was a little girl.'

'So just the two of you?'

'Yes.' She turned and came across the kitchen with a quick step, stopping beside Pierre. 'Please. You must listen. I want to take Papi to England. I have an aunt there. She would look after him. I am going to train as a wireless operator. Then I'll come back and work for the Resistance!'

Pierre watched her as she talked, moving backwards and forwards from the range, laying dishes, stirring soup, all with the same fierce intensity. He caught sight of her hands, as she came to the table. Tiny hands, fine, the wrists white and slim, but the hands scarred; new scars.

'What happened to your hands?'

'It's the bloody winch. On the boat. In the winter, when it's icy. It runs away sometimes.'

'You fish by yourself?'

'Of course. Who else would do it? Anyway, I love the sea. I grew up beside it.'

A sudden stillness in the kitchen, light filtering through the long window at one end, a flame leaping in the range where she had placed a new log, how it cast a little glow in the sadness of the room. How her hands lay like small white birds, broken-winged, between one dead 'toc' of the clock and the next; another time, unmeasured.

'Enough of that!' she said briskly. 'It's not important. You must hear the rest of my plan. Because we're close to the *Zone Interdit*, and I always fish along the Wall, I can help you. They're used to me being there. We can make drawings together. We'll find out things for the British War Office. Then they'll be so grateful, they'll bring me to England!'

'I never heard such nonsense!' the old man grumbled. 'We're safe here. Got a nice little set-up. No one will bother us. I'm not going back to England. It's full of rats!'

'Don't take any notice of him! He's confused since Grandmamma died. Do you know that there is no radio operator closer than Château-le-Vigny? The *reseau* has to get a courier all the way down there to send a message. No wonder things go wrong. I could help, if they trained me and sent me back here. I know I could do it!'

Pierre nodded. There was no point telling her that they would never send her back to her 'home' area.

'A radio operator is the most dangerous job,' he said. 'They get taken out all the time.'

'I don't care! Promise me you'll tell them. I've asked the others, but it will mean more if you tell them. Now you've seen the situation. Just pass on the message. It's not much to ask!'

The old man sat up suddenly, his blind eyes staring.

'Has the British agent come?'

Rebecca came back to the table, leaning over. 'Yes! He's here. He's called Jean. We mustn't tell anyone. No one!'

'Not even Jacques?'

'No, not even Jacques!'

'I'm worried about being here,' Pierre said. 'I'm putting you all in danger. If I'm found here, you'll be shot. Both of you! I should move on.'

She turned on him.

'You can't go! We'll keep quiet, I promise! Papi won't tell anyone. I'll see to it. As for the danger, it's nothing to us.' In the dim light, her face was white.

'Promise me! I mean to go to England. I mean to be a radio operator. What do they call it in your bloody slang? A "pianist"! I'll be a "pianist". I'll come back. I'll be the best in France. They'll never catch me.'

5

He wasn't what she expected. Quiet, quite shy. And young —
not much older than her. He had nice eyes, she thought. Hair
cut *en brosse,* like a worker. It was hard to know who he really
was. It was confusing, all that stuff about code names. What was
his real name? And where did he come from? He looked the part
of a worker, but she wanted to tell him his French was too good.
Posh like an aristocrat. Like the Count up at the château, who
had committed suicide after his son had been taken to the STO
and was killed soon after. He was quite serious. She supposed
it was a big responsibility being a British agent. Maybe he was
afraid. And they all wanted miracles from him. Anyway, for all
his good papers, she hoped he wasn't picked up by the Gestapo,
or they would know at once he was a fake.

***

Pierre was dreaming he was there again. The ship was sinking,
stern first. The lights were burning on all the upper decks, but
there was no one left aboard. They all managed to get into the
life rafts, but some of them hadn't got lifejackets. There hadn't
been time. Fire was beginning to lick along the hull, from bow
to stern.

They looked back at the ship.

'Jesus Christ!' Bill said. 'Look at that! Oil in the sea. We'll go
up like a fucking torch!'

It was not yet dark, and perhaps they'd get picked up soon.
There had been just time to send out a Mayday call after she
was hit.

'Come on Frenchie! Get on with it.' Bill shouted at him.
'Paddle for all your worth. Unless you want to end up like one
of them flaming pancakes you're always on about.'

There were six of them in the raft, and they were all paddling like hell through the stinking stuff the ship was pumping out. Then, like some great whale, with a sigh, a rush of wind, she was below the waves, slipping away almost without sound.

'Bloody U-Boats. Slimy bastards,' someone shouted. 'Always sneaking around. I felt both them torpedoes down in the engine room. We've been lucky to get out.'

'Save your breath,' Bill said. 'Just paddle and make as much noise as you can.'

Other naval vessels were near, they knew, and the Merchant Navy ships they were escorting. It wouldn't be long.

But then the great wave hit; the last revenge of the ship going down. The life raft flipped, spilling them in the sea.

'Archimedes' fucking principle!' Bill gasped, in the water. 'I always thought it would get me in the end.'

They were clinging to each other. He tried to support them both in the sea, hanging on to the upturned raft with one hand. There was oil all around. Others were calling out, screaming. He hung onto Bill's jacket, trying to breathe, trying to keep his face out of the oil. Another huge wave hit, but this time, miraculously, it flipped their raft.

'Come on, Bill, just hang on here.' He scrabbled for the side rail. Someone grabbed his back and tried to haul him into the raft. He tried to pull Bill up with him, but he was a dead weight, slipping away into the ink black water, out of sight.

Someone in the raft was holding onto his uniform. He ducked his head under the black stuff, searching for Bill. There was no light. He was trying to hold his breath, but then he had to come up for air. He felt oil flood his throat. He began to choke.

***

She heard him at the far end of the house, shouting in English.

'Bill! The boat! The boat's gone down!'

If anyone heard him shouting, they would know straight away. She grabbed the jug from beside the stove, filled it with hot water, and ran up the stairs.

'You were shouting about a ship!' she said. 'In English! Do you often shout like that?'

'How do I know? I was asleep.'

'If you do, it's better you are a long way from other people.'

He started to climb out of bed. The girl put the jug down hurriedly and turned to the door.

'Grandfather understands it all now,' she said at the door. 'I've explained everything — what we have to tell people about you being his great-nephew, helping with the boat, all that.'

'I'm glad. I was worried.'

'Even if he seems to get confused, it doesn't mean anything. You mustn't fret. Underneath he knows about the danger and he won't tell anyone. It's just that ... the top part of his mind is muddled. He was what they called an Onion Johnny, you know. Only he's English really, not French. He married my grandmother before the First World War, and he's lived here ever since. So he's on your side.'

'Thank you. It's helpful to know.'

'He misses England, though he's never been back since ... the onions. Will it matter if he talks about it sometimes?'

'Of course not. If we're alone, it's fine.'

She was standing with her hand on the latch of the open door, as though she were afraid he might try to get out of bed again. There was a flush of colour along her cheekbones.

'I'll bring you some pyjamas,' she said. 'Papi has spare ones.'

He put one leg out of the bed, the sheet wrapped around his middle.

'Thank you. We have to travel light!'

She turned away again without smiling. He heard her footsteps clanging on the wooden stairs.

When he got downstairs the old man was already at the table, sucking his bread. Rebecca clattered about the kitchen, passing through the long light from the window. She laid a bowl of coffee in front of him, and there were eggs in a blue dish. The coffee tasted of bitter acorns.

The old man leaned across the table.

'She ain't fishin' today because of you!'

Pierre looked at Rebecca. 'I can get my own breakfast. You don't have to look after me.'

She nodded, her head on one side as she poured more coffee into his bowl.

'Tomorrow I'll go fishing. But today I'll just go to the market and help Monsieur Dadier with his stall. You'll soon get used to my routine. But in the day, you must cope by yourself.'

'Of course. I'll be busy anyway.'

'I'm sorry. I've got to go.'

She swept the plates from the table with an impatient gesture, leaving the old man dropping crumbs. Then she was gone.

'That don't do to cross her,' the old man said.

The room seemed suddenly close and dark. He thought about the contacts he had to make that day, how he wanted to be out of the room, in the fresh air. It felt like a trap. He went outside. Rebecca was standing in the yard, lifting the loop of her apron over her head in a slow gesture which threw her hair over her face. She flung it back with a shake, like a snake sloughing off a skin. She walked across the yard into the barn.

After a minute he followed her. There was a battered Renault van standing just inside — a *gazo* fitted with charcoal burners. She was muttering to herself, struggling to get the charcoal to ignite. There had been a frost in the night. Even in the barn their breath steamed in the air. In the shadows, ice was blue on the cobbles.

She turned to him.

'Tell me about your family. Where you come from? Why do you speak French so well?'

'You know I can't. If I'm caught, they'll interrogate you.'

'We know so little about you. That's how we get to know people, isn't it? Knowing where they're from, who their families are? You ought to know you sound like an aristocrat, well, posh anyway. It's no good speaking French so well; if it's *too* good … it's too … Parisien! You'll stand out in the marketplace. They should have sent you looking smart, not like a peasant. Anyway, you need to know.'

'I'd stick out even more if I was dressed like some kind of minor aristocrat! I'm not that kind of person. You've got it wrong.'

'Perhaps if you're lucky the Germans may not pick it up, but the French will. And some of them won't be on your side. I'm just telling you for your own good.'

'I could help you with the fishing,' he said. 'It would be a good way of getting round the countryside without anyone suspecting me. Then you could teach me to speak like a peasant while we're in the boat!'

She looked at him angrily. Then realised he was teasing. For a moment she almost smiled.

'It's not funny!'

He wanted to tell her about Bill, and the ship going down. About who he really was, about growing up in France, and how it felt coming back. There was something about her. Those fierce brown eyes, pale face, hair caught like fire in the sun, or like now, in the shadow of the barn, still that colour cascading down her back. He wanted to say *One day, maybe after the war, I can tell you about my family. I'll tell you my real name, where I come from.* But he knew having those feelings was very dangerous.

The *gazo* ignited in a blast of black smoke. He watched her drive away. Then he went back into the kitchen, where the old man sat, his hands flat on the table, eyes straining for sound. The kitchen was dim and cold. Claustrophobic. The old man with his crumbling memories, the girl, disturbed, fiery, playing her own game.

'I know about you, boy,' the old man said suddenly. 'Don't you think I'm a fool. You can rely on old Thomas. I seen a few things. I nivver learned much of the lingo, even after all these years. Keep meself to meself, see. Only Jacques, the postie, him and me is mates. Who'd a thought it? But I ain't tellin' no one. They're all Frenchies at heart, friends of the Boches. Don't do ter trust them.'

It would be a slow business, he thought, building trust. Not all action. Cycling round the countryside, day after day, building up the network, extending the *reseau* with cautious tact, sitting in dark rooms with glasses of *marc* and Calvados while the long clocks ticked on. He would have to find new fields for *le parachutage*, send messages to Château-Le-Vigny, hold back the impatience of the new resisters for open war, train new men with the plastic explosive, a sick headache from the almond smell in a hot room, too much sour wine. All the time he would have to make decisions, and because he was *l'agent de l'intelligence* (and maybe a friend of Winston Churchill) they would trust him and believe in him, till the end.

6

After those first days it became a pattern of their nights that they would wait together for Rebecca. Pierre would light the lamp. Sometimes they would have a glass of Calvados. The old man would tell him, in English, about the creek on the East Coast where he was brought up, and about his brother Matthew who was killed in the Great War, buried on the Somme. How he had become a partner in a Brittany crabber after he married a girl from the Îsles de Glénan, and how they had had one son, who had become a doctor. Rebecca's father, killed, alongside her mother, a nurse at the same hospital, when the Germans bombed it in the first days of the war.

Rebecca would come back with a basket of prawns or a bag of whelks, once a few sole from her fishing, seafood left over from the market. She would move swiftly about the room, in and out of the shadows, bringing the crock of butter to the table and the dark bread, sometimes wine from the café in the square in Sainte Croix. They would eat hungrily, listening to her news from the town and messages from Paul when he could not come himself, how the Major from the command post had requisitioned all the lobster and no one would dare to ask for the money, because the Commandant was giving a celebration for the *collaborateurs* who might otherwise be getting cold feet, the way the war was going for the Boches.

Two days a week Rebecca would stay at home from fishing and bake the dark sour bread which drove her to despair, and do the chores on the farm. Every day Jacques, the postman, a new member of the *reseau*, would walk three times up the lane to see his friend and milk the cows morning and evening. At twelve o'clock he would come to feed Thomas and share his meal. Little Jacques was very useful, with his sly gossip, eyes everywhere. Sometimes Thomas would go to meet him down the lane. Pierre would see them sometimes as he was riding back on his bicycle, Thomas feeling with his stick for the huge potholes in the road and Jacques, his empty mailbag over his arm, a cheese or a cabbage on the handlebars of his bicycle, dancing behind the old man, his sharp little voice squeaking with laughter at his own jokes.

December was hard. Pierre was still at the farm and things seemed safe. There was ice in the ruts. Hunger drove people to despair. There were two suicides in Sainte Croix that month. The curé refused to bury them in consecrated ground. He preached the party line from the bishops, that they should co-operate with the Germans, and he had introduced a special prayer for le Maréchal.

Deliver us from evil, O Marshal of France! He has suppressed the freemasons and taken power from the anti-patriotic and the anti-religious! Vive le Maréchal!

They were in a farming district, protected from the worst of the famine which ebbed the will of the French as surely as a slow poison. But the old still suffered — he found an old woman lying in the road on the way to Very-les-Bains, too weak to walk the last two miles to the village. He carried her on his bicycle to her grandson's house in the Rue Molière.

They were all short of fuel. Every trip now Pierre collected wood for the range, balanced on the handlebars of his bicycle. When Rebecca came back home in the evening in the *gazo*, she had done the same. Many people cooked over oil drums with rolled-up balls of newspaper. Fallen timber was scavenged as soon as it fell, its bones picked clean by old women, their faces crow-like with hunger. There was nothing to spare.

Yet everywhere Pierre went, every house and farm he visited, there would be fresh bread and farm butter, a trenche of fat meat for the British agent and often a glass of precious *marc* saved for the Liberation.

The farm was ideally suited, well off the beaten track, having two exits. It was close to the sea, and the *Zone Interdit*, which was dangerous, but otherwise good; fairly central for Château-Le-Vigny, and his own spreading network. Nevertheless, Pierre knew he shouldn't stay too long. A drop had been agreed by London. The weather over that part of France was pretty bad during the moon period, and a lot of low cloud over Europe. He had a *message personnel* to listen for on the BBC's *Les Français Parlent aux Français*, but nothing came.

They celebrated Christmas at the farm with two old chickens roasted in the range. Jacques came in the afternoon and the three of them drank two bottles of eau de vie, much to Rebecca's fury.

There had been a message from London about Rebecca — full of *gp mutts*, deliberate mistakes to show the message was genuine. He had kept his promise. He was to get her out in the next few weeks if he could. It might mean going to Michel (Houseboat reseau) who had experience of picking Lysander fields, and arranging a pick up. SOE were desperate to train more W/T operators. Another of the 'pianists' in his area had been taken. It happened all the time. He didn't tell Rebecca, but he knew he would have to, soon.

7

Just before dawn, Pierre found her crying in the yard. It had rained in the night and it was frozen into a skin of ice, rutted and treacherous. She had one of the fishing nets spread around her feet.

'What is it?'

'That stupid old man. Look at this net! For God's sake, I can't do anything with it. He keeps saying he can mend the nets. But look at it!'

'He's blind! Don't be too hard on him.'

'Don't make excuses for him. It's his job. I need him to do it. He falls asleep, and the nets end up like this!'

He picked up the corner of the net and poked a finger through the mesh, wondering how she managed to catch anything.

'I'll come with you this morning. I've got nothing better to do. I'm waiting for a message.'

'There's no need. I can manage.' Rebecca gathered up the net. 'Anyway I'm OK now. Sorry I blew my top!'

'I'm supposed to be here to help you with the boat,' he said. 'I haven't done anything so far. It must look suspicious ... if anyone's watching.'

Rebecca walked towards the barn, trailing the net with its cork floats over the icy ground.

'Well, I'm going now. If you want to come, you'll have to hurry!'

Pierre followed. 'OK. It would help to have a look at the coast. I had a signal about it months ago.'

'It means going into the *Zone Interdit*. Isn't that dangerous for you?'

'I've got a pass. Anyway, my papers are real enough.'

'I guess you can come if you like.'

They went in the *gazo*, turning down the lane which led to the sea. There, below them, was that gun emplacement. There was a patrol on the clifftop. Rebecca shifted down a gear and roared forward.

'It'll be OK. Don't worry.'

A young officer, an Oberleutnant, held up his arm. They screeched to a halt. He leaned in Rebecca's open window, his breath steaming in the cold. He was very young, blue eyes under his cap.

'So this is the nephew?'

'Great-nephew,' Rebecca smiled back, one white hand with its broken nails resting on the wheel.

'Bonjour!' Pierre tried to sound casual.

'He will help you with the fishing? It's a tough job!' The officer looked at her anxiously.

'Of course! That's what he's here for! And he's recovering from TB. The sea air will be good for him.' Rebecca twisted a strand of hair.

'Very good!' he smiled again, waving them on.

'Bastard Schleuhs!' she muttered, when they were out of sight. 'Actually, he's not bad. For a bloody German, anyway.'

'I didn't know about the TB.'

'I just made it up. So they don't take you for the STO. And they might wonder why you haven't gone already. It's obvious. You should have thought of it.'

The small fishing boat was anchored in a cove just beyond the headland, where there was no access from the shore. She always referred to it as a trawler, but it was really an open dayboat, roughly fitted out to take drift nets. No engine. In any case it would have been useless without fuel.

They rowed out in an ancient clinker-built dinghy which leaked. He wondered how she managed in high winds, how she dragged the heavy tender down the beach on her own.

'How do you manage when the weather's bad?'

'I manage. I have to.'

There was a small hand winch in the bow. Rebecca went forward and began to crank it, pulling on the anchor chain. The boat swung to her mooring, jibbing at the tide. Pierre knew enough not to offer to help. There were sheets coiled on the side deck, worn fibres bristled with salt frost where they lay in the shadow. He thought of that cruel winch with its teeth, the ice sloughing off onto the deck.

It was one of those hard blue days, a stabbing wind coming across a white sea; cat's paws of wind which stung but left the sails slack. Rebecca stood by the wheel amidships. He watched the beach, trying to memorise everything; the gun emplacements, the wire. Now the tide was low enough to expose them, he could see the spikes and crosses between the tides, designed to rip the bottom out of any landing craft. They reminded him of games of jackstones when he was young, a giant game flung onto the beach.

Once they came quite close in and he could see the Wall, men of the Todt he had been briefed about, toiling in their brown uniforms. Rusting rods sprang out of the concrete. And there were others, their feet bound with bloody cloths, skeletal creatures who picked their way among the half-finished blocks, hacking at the clay.

'Russian prisoners,' Rebecca said quietly. 'I feel sorry for them. The Germans work them till they die. Klaus, that officer, he calls them "scum". He says they are beneath contempt.' She squinted up at the sail. 'Everyone knows the prisoners are mixing stuff with the concrete, and messing up the proportion of sand. It's a standing joke.'

'Under the eyes of the German patrols?'

'Why should they care? They're dead anyway. Once the first big storm comes, the Wall will start cracking. You'll see. It's started already, further down the coast. The village takes food for them, gets it to them somehow when they can. Even though everyone is short. The Russians used to be our enemies. Now we feel sorry for them.'

She shot the drift net, taking advantage of the first of the flood to drift back along the bay. There wasn't much of a catch when they pulled it in. Then they lifted several lobster creels, separating crab from lobster. He took the wheel, braced against the wheelhouse.

'You seem at home in a boat,' she said. 'Were you in the Navy? You know, in Britain?' Rebecca didn't miss much.

'You know I can't talk about it' he said, thinking about the ship going down. 'Anyway, you've got some good crabs. You should be pleased.'

'I guess. It's the lobster that make money. The German officers like them. They pay good prices, if they ever pay, and it keeps us going at the farm.' She dangled a lobster in front of him, its claws flailing wildly.

'You've heard from London,' she said.

'Who told you?'

'Paul.'

'He shouldn't have done.'

'He thought I knew. Of course, he did. Why didn't you tell me?'

'There's nothing definite. I didn't want to get your hopes up. If there had been any news, I would have told you. It could be a Lysander pick up, but the trouble is, they're short of Lysanders. You'll have to be patient. It could be a while.'

Rebecca lifted each crab and the blue lobsters, putting them in their separate baskets.

'I don't think you take me seriously,' she said at last. 'You still don't know that I'm always serious about everything important. Serious enough to leave Papi behind, if I have to!' She was crouching over the basket, her head bent.

'I'm sorry,' he said. 'Perhaps we'll hear soon, and then you can go to England. I can't stay at the farm much longer, anyway.'

'Papi told lies for me, because Grandmamma was Jewish. Did you know that? He saved me from the Boche. Even after all this time, he doesn't really like the French, but he went to Armand's father, and asked for false papers for me, so that I wouldn't have to register. He saved my life. Now I may have to leave him behind, if he won't leave. That's how serious I am!'

'I should have told you.'

'There's something else too!' she said, leaning forward. 'Ever since they began to build the Wall in this sector, I've made sketches of every stage. I've got all the measurements. The emplacements, the exact position of the minefields. If they'll take me to England straight away, I can show them. There are people watching on this coast — ordinary people reporting to Armand and others. The sketches aren't unique. But they'll be useful.'

'I'm afraid it won't make much difference to when they bring you out,' he said. 'The Lysander pick up already has a high priority. London is desperate for fluent French-speaking W/T operators. The casualty rate's very high. You must know that.'

Rebecca flung her head back and stared at the sky, hands clenched into fists.

'Aaah! I can't stand it. If only they'd let me do something!'

Far overhead a bomber crossed the coast, the throb like a sick headache. The sails bellied and slackened.

'Just try to be patient! Michel already sent the co-ordinates for a Lysander field to London. The same is happening all over France.'

Rebecca said nothing, bending her head again to clear seaweed from the scuppers, chucking it into the sea.

***

He had lied to me, she thought, or at least not told me the truth. How many other lies had he told? Nothing was as it seemed in this bloody war.

33

8

It was late morning when they got to the market — a few stalls scattered along the Quai Maritime. Some stallholders were packing up already, having sold their fish. Easy to sell anything in wartime France, if you could get it.

Everyone knew Rebecca. Several old women, thin-faced, began to queue for the mackerel. A Major from the Wehrmacht appeared, and the queue melted away. He took the three lobster.

'I have my bill here,' Rebecca said. 'For the last month. All the lobsters I'm owed.'

'Sorry, Mademoiselle.' He bowed stiffly. 'It's nothing to do with me. You had better send the bill to the Kommandant.'

'How often does that happen?' Pierre asked, as the queue began to drift back.

'They usually pay up in the end. It depends.' Rebecca took an old woman's oilcloth bag and picked out a crab for her.

The old woman grabbed the bag back. She grinned toothlessly up at him.

'Lobster is not for the likes of us! She can make more from the Boches!'

Rebecca flushed.

'Who cares if it's the Boches,' she said softly to the woman's back, as she clattered away over the cobbles. 'I'll have payment soon enough!'

He saw Paul, the courier, helping on one of the stalls at the far end. He was with a tall, thin youth, with a drooping moustache, his brother Armand.

'There's Paul,' Pierre said. 'I need to talk to him.'

He left Rebecca and walked down the length of the quay, the stone slippery with fish scales. Armand was haggling about the price of mackerel.

'Every week, Madame, you tell me I've raised my prices. God knows, there would be excuse enough, with the shortages and the Boches with their damned regulations. But I'm a patriotic Frenchman. I would rather send my best man to the *travail* before I'd rob my own countrywoman.'

The woman was middle-aged, gaunt. She looked at him sourly.

'Your kind make me sick!' she spat. 'Consorting with criminals. Disobeying the Maréchal. I should report you! I know what you get up to. It's a disgrace. I'd be ashamed if a son of mine were such a bad Catholic!'

She snatched the mackerel and slapped them into her basket. When she had stomped off, Armand gave a rueful shrug.

'What can one do about such patriotism?'

It was Pierre's brief to give support to any political group which might help to free France, whether Gaullist or FTP (the Communists). Armand was the leader of a strong group of Gaullists around Sainte Croix — the forces of the Free French; the BCRA. They were the 'other firm' and relations between the two London-based operations were often strained. But here in the field they helped each other when they could. But it was hard to keep out of politics. It was all around.

Paul was stacking fish baskets. He looked up at his brother.

'I keep telling Armand he's a fool! Everyone in Sainte Croix knows he's working for the Gaullists. Yesterday a young man came into the shop, from Cuilly, would you believe, twenty miles away at least! He asked for Armand. Wants to fight for the Free French! On the run from the STO. For God's sake!'

'Paul, I need to talk to you,' Pierre said. 'Can you spare a few minutes?'

'Sure, sure, we were just packing up to go to Louis' place. Why don't you come?'

Pierre knew the café in the square. It was a dangerous rendezvous, a meeting point for all kinds of 'resisters'. Some of them were the loud-mouthed sort.

'Couldn't we meet somewhere else?'

The brothers stared at him in horror.

'And miss the *plat du jour*?' Armand shook his head. 'Today's Wednesday. If you can get it, it is always *tripes* on Wednesday. Miss the *tripes*? You must be mad!'

'OK. But I'll have to tell Rebecca where I'll be. I'll join you in a few minutes.'

Rebecca was not by her stall. Dadier was minding it. He told him she'd gone to Madame Monier's house.

'She takes fish to her every Wednesday. She's crippled, you see. Can't get out. She won't be back till after lunch.'

'Can you tell her I'll be at Louis' place?'

Just then, a small boy, dressed in a pair of adult's underpants and a tweed jacket, slipped round the corner by the épicerie, and grabbed a fish by its tail from Rebecca's stall. He dashed away across the slimy cobbles.

'Hey! Come back here, you little bugger!'

Dadier gave half-hearted chase and came back.

'The kids have gone to the dogs. But what can you do? It's the war!' He shrugged. 'Don't worry. I'll tell Rebecca.'

Pierre walked down the Boulevard des Plantes into the main square. Louis' bar tabac had the usual tables spilling out into the square. He thought that even if there were such a creature as a half-witted Gestapo agent, it wouldn't take him very long to spot that this was a centre of the local Résistance. Conspicuous young men in black berets and zip leather jackets stood half in the roadway, arguing violently. Others threaded between the tables, embracing. It was like a bad film of the Spanish Civil War, the glamorous picture of Résistance, the one that Hollywood might have liked. Not the true one. The miracle was that the café hadn't been raided.

He spotted Paul and Armand at the far end of the bar. Strains of a patriotic song floated out from the inner room, followed by a shout. Armand threaded his way through the crush at the rear of the bar and disappeared through a door. Paul looked up and saw him.

'Ah! The *tripes* are on. What luck, eh? I've ordered for you. And there's some good wine today. Special customers, see. You don't get this service everywhere.'

'Sorry,' Pierre said. 'I need to talk to you. Can we go somewhere quiet, just for a few minutes?'

'But what about the bloody *tripes*? I've been looking forward to those all day. Let's be quick!'

They walked out of the bar, past the old men in the corner playing *belote*. Louis, impassive, was washing the ash from the *zinc* with a cloth, dropping more from the end of his cigarette.

They turned the corner into one of the alleyways which radiated off the square. A smell of urine, a mangy dog lying in the sun. It was warm there, out of the wind. A woman in black, her hair tied back in a scarf, paused from beating a carpet on the balcony. She stared at them standing at her open doorway. A smell of onions from the dark kitchen beyond.

'Mother of God!' Paul exploded. 'What the hell's the matter? You're as jumpy as a hen with the shits!'

'Hey, you!' A voice came from above. The old woman was leaning over the balcony, a chamber pot in one hand, the other brawny arm laid along the ironwork.

'Move along or you'll get this pisspot on your heads!'

'I need to talk about Rebecca, and the drop,' Pierre said. 'It could be any time! You'll have to get a message back to the group.'

A black Citroen screeched round the corner from the direction of the port, narrowly missing an old man on a bike. It was closely followed by a second. Its tyres screaming, it buffeted from one side of the pavement to the other. He caught sight of a fat man sitting in the back of the second car, expressionless, homburg planted over a squat face.

Pierre gripped Paul's shoulder, to stop him running back. After the cars, the street was very still. Then one shot. A scream. A shout.

All along the street, doors were shutting. A girl with a baby carriage ran across the road in front of them.

They stood in the doorway of the *coiffure*. The fruitier came to the door of his shop opposite. He dragged a box of peaches towards the entrance. But before he could reach the doorway, a truck came round the corner from the direction of the port, packed with troops. It knocked the peaches flying. An overhead sign fell in a cloud of dust.

There was more noise now from the direction of the square. Several more shots. A man ran out of the alleyway. He paused, hands braced on either side of the broken stonework, looking frantically from left to right, sweat on his stubbled chin.

'That's Jean-François! He's in the group!' Paul whispered. The man ran across the road and hammered on the door of the pawnbrokers. The door stayed shut.

He ran back into the centre of the road, held in a streak of sun. A clatter of boots, a shout, two shots. The man stretched up his arms to the rectangle of sky above the rooftops, then fell back. Further down, the tray of peaches littered the road, their red flesh coating the cobbles.

Dust lay on the sunny air. Two German soldiers ran down the street and dragged the body away. Pierre and Paul pressed back into the doorway. The cyclist picked his bicycle out of the roadway, straightened the front wheel and zig-zagged off across the slippery cobbles. The peaches lay on the dust. The fruitier ran out to grab a peach which lay uncrushed in the gutter.

'Him and his fucking peaches,' Paul muttered. 'Only the Schleuhs can afford them. I've got to go back! I'm worried about Armand!'

'Wait for the Schleuhs to go, then we'll go down. They may only have been looking for *refractaires*. He could be OK.'

'No chance. Half the town knows he's a Lieutenant in the FFI.'

Doors had begun to open on the street. Just then the truck racketed past once again, this time crowded with civilian prisoners. The doors open, dark cracks, eyes looked out. The two Citroens drove past, very fast, their blinds down, yellow-faced wheels swinging from side to side on the cobbles. The dust settled on the air again.

The sun had shifted a little, the corner now in shadow. The door of the florist's shop opened slowly, and a young woman came out, holding a bunch of freesias. She stood for a moment, looking up and down the street. Then she stepped over the smeared peaches, walking to the centre of the road where there was a darker stain. Lifting her hands, she scattered the flowers on the ground.

A girl in a red skirt came out of the gown shop across the road and began to clean the windows. A stream of water ran onto her skirt onto the dusty pavement. The pawnbroker unlocked the door and looked up and down the street.

'Give me your tobacco tin!' Pierre whispered.

'What the hell for?'

'Just do it. Watch me!'

He opened the tin and shuffled along the pavement, head bowed. Every once in a while, he would find a fag end and drop it into the tin. Paul copied him. No one looked at them. It was a common enough sight.

The café doors were closed, chairs tipped over on the cobbles. Coffee spilled on the pavement; a red stain threaded between the stones. Two *Miliciens* stood by the entrance to the café, talking and laughing. He could smell the aroma of Russian tobacco. Rich. Expensive. Occasionally the *Miliciens* shouted at a workman who was boarding up the broken window, telling him to hurry up.

They shuffled back into the alley, stopping under the same balcony as before. The woman with the pisspot was standing by the door. Paul was being sick in the sloping drain. She watched him for a few moments. Then she disappeared inside, coming out with a bottle of cognac, glasses, and a bowl of water. Paul was slumped against the wall. The woman dipped her hand in the bowl and wiped Paul's face, poured out a measure of cognac.

'Here, Monsieur! You too!' She handed him a glass. 'You're as white as a sheet. Don't you start being sick in my drain as well. I've got to clear that lot up.'

'Merci, Madame. You're very kind. Did you see the raid?'

'Ah oui, Monsieur. I saw everything from my balcony. They've taken Louis and some of the young men, and a young girl too. A terrible sight. Two of the young men tried to run into this place. They shot them in front of the others. And there was another. They're saying he ran away and was shot.'

'Yes, that's true. We saw it,' Pierre said. 'Did you see a young man with a long moustache, black hair?'

'I know him! He always wears a red smock! He's in the square in the mornings...' She peered down at Paul. 'I recognise you now. You're his brother!'

Paul struggled to his feet.

'Do you know? Was he taken?'

'Yes, yes, I'm afraid so. In the Citroen. Eight others, maybe more, in the truck. And that young woman, not much more than a girl! Such a thin thing in those silly trousers. I can't imagine what La Geste would want with her. Well, I can, but it's too dreadful to think about!'

A pigeon jinked through the alleyway, blundering into the afternoon shadow, under the black clothes drying in lines across the balconies. Soaring up at last, gold and blue in the January sun.

'The girl? Did she have red hair?'

'Oui, oui, Monsieur. I know her too! She has a fish stall in the market. A nice girl, always asks a fair price.'

Pierre ran down the alleyway, where the drain water had carved channels in the stone. The tall houses leaned over, with their snatches of talk, smells of late afternoons in winter. Old women in their black lacy scarves were standing in doorways. He dodged a group of children playing at war. *Ak Ak Ak*, with broken bits of wood.

M. Dadier was packing up Rebecca's stall. He looked up with a smile.

'Ah! So glad you're safe! Rebecca came to find you in the café. Then when I heard what happened there, I was concerned...'

'She was taken!'

Dadier slumped on a trestle, his head in his hands.

'Oh, God! It was my fault! She came back from Madame Monier. Madame's ill, Rebecca couldn't eat with her. It seemed natural to persuade her to come to the café. After all, the *tripes* are excellent.'

Paul arrived. He still looked bad.

'Don't go home, Paul. It's not safe. Can you cycle up to Château-Le-Vigny? They have to know about the raid.'

'What about Armand? He's always so careless, damn him!'

'Concentrate now! I'm not writing it down.'

He was loading the last baskets into the *gazo* when Paul came back again.

'My head's full of wool. How could I forget? I'm a bloody fool. I had a message for you.'

'Tell me!'

'The *parachutage* for Very-les Bains will be in the next moon.' He spoke like an automaton. 'A Lysander pick up has been scheduled for the same moon if possible, maybe a day, two days later. They didn't say.'

Rebecca would be able to get out ... if they let her go. But what were the chances?

'Paul, listen! Ask them to wait for further messages. Not do anything till they've heard from you!'

Had any of their own group been taken, apart from Rebecca?

'Tell Michel everything!' he said. 'Ask him to compose a message to London. Don't forget!'

It was clear he had to get away from Sainte Croix, and *Le Tamaris*. Almost everyone talked to La Geste in the end. Almost everyone.

9

People on the pavement looked away. As though they were already dead.

'Why did Jean leave in such a hurry?' Armand whispered to her, as they were lining up.

He had lied to her once, or at least not told her everything. Could he be trusted?

The fat man from the Citroen was staring at her. Looking her up and down, wet lips, a pink tongue. They had been taken to the big house on the edge of town. Everyone knew what went on there.

'Papers, pretty girl! What were you doing in the town? Are you a *gonzesse*? A little tart? You could do well. I would pay to have you any time.'

A chorus of voices from the room.

'Leave her alone! She has a stall on the market.'

'She's an orphan. She supplies the High Command with fish. Let her go!'

Rebecca swallowed back tears. There was no way she was going to cry in front of him, the snake. But her papers were false.

She took a deep breath.

'Perhaps you would take me to the Kommandant? I supply lobster to the Kommandant every week from my stall. The best lobster in the market. He owes me for a month's supply. Here! I have my bill!' She stared at him defiantly. 'I'm sure he wouldn't want to be in debt to me. After all, the Germans are known to be so honourable.' She felt sickness rise in her throat. 'I need the money. I support my grandfather and myself; he's blind. As the Occupying Forces, you are responsible for our welfare.'

Just then the dark kitchen, with Papi fussing over the nets, seemed the best place in the world. She would never be angry with him again.

He was staring at her. The others in the room were quiet. It would be their turn next. Once more he looked down at her papers. She felt her stomach clench. An SS officer she recognised from the market stepped forward, saluted, and spoke to him in a whisper. He looked at her.

'The Unterscharfuhrer tells me he has seen you in the market, when he bought lobster for the Kommandant. And, yes, I have seen you myself, now I think about it. I have even eaten your lobster occasionally with the Kommandant. Delicious. You are such a pretty girl. You would grace our table. Yes, delicious. I must mention you, but for now I will take the bill. Be assured, I will make sure it reaches him, and you will be paid. As you say, we Germans are honourable people.'

She tried to keep her face blank. Once more his tongue flickered over his lips, a fat lizard. He clicked his heels.

'Heil Hitler!' She tried not to flinch at the salute, so close to her face.

'You may leave. But I will certainly mention you to the Kommandant. You will be paid for your services ... whatever they may be. I will send you an invitation to our next little evening. It will be amusing.'

A soldier took her from the room and down the stairs. She kept her eyes on the floor, not daring to look at the others. From above her, in a room somewhere, someone was screaming.

***

It was clear that whether Rebecca returned or not, Pierre would have to leave *Le Tamaris*.

He hid the *gazo* a few hundred metres from the farm, in a copse just off the road. He wasn't sure of the reception he might find. If all was well, he would leave as soon as it was dark.

The old man was sitting in his chair, making a mess of a net. He cried out at once when he heard his footsteps, knowing something was wrong. Pierre went over to the range and ladled water into the coffee pot. The fire had gone out in the oven and he went outside to fetch more wood.

He made coffee for them both, and heated the fish stew which Rebecca had left in the arrière-cuisine. He told the old man what had happened. Everything seemed calm.

But Rebecca might talk.

A curious kind of fatalism crept over him. Was this what happened before people got caught? That's what everybody said. If Rebecca had talked, La Geste might come for them any time. He knew he should go immediately and leave the old man sighing over his bread.

The recruiting officer had been a bad judge of character. If he ever got back to England, he would tell him why. He had broken the rules. No emotional involvement.

Thomas rose halfway through the meal and felt his way over to the *chiffonier* in the hallway. He came back with a bottle of green liquid. They drank the cider together, right down to the swirling depths, where the cobwebs seemed to lie. He wanted to tell Thomas he had to leave, to go with them to Château-Le-Vigny in the *gazo*. There he would be safe. But instead he fell asleep with his head on the table.

When he woke it was dark. There was a noise in the hallway. He got up without scraping the chair and moved silently to the side of the cupboard. The hiss of a match. A sudden leap of light under the half-open door. He remembered his gun was in his room. He rarely carried it. It was too much of a risk if he were stopped. The door opened slowly. He lifted his arm. The candle flared backwards in the draught. He saw the small white hand.

'Rebecca! You bloody fool! I nearly killed you.'

The gun was in her other hand, pointing at him.

'They said in the café you knew the raid was coming. You ran away in a hurry and left Armand to be taken. Some people believe you are working for the Boches.'

She lifted the candle in its saucer and the liquid wax shivered. Her face looked yellow in the light, and there were lines etched deeply around her nose. The gun didn't move.

'I don't want to believe them, but why did you leave?' Rebecca said. 'First, I thought you'd been taken in the Citroen with Armand. They took him to Caen. The Gestapo will torture him. It would be better if he had been shot. Then I heard the things the others were saying, that you and Paul had run away.'

'What do you think?'

She stood looking at him in the candlelight, uncertain.

He spoke carefully, choosing his words.

'I had a feeling the café was a dangerous place. There's often a reason.'

'So it was intuition? You could have saved Armand!'

'I couldn't do anything. Do you think I would have let you be taken too?'

Rebecca was staring at him. At last, she lowered the gun, slipping it into the front pocket of her smock. He heard the click of the safety catch. He wondered if it was loaded, how she had got hold of it. She pushed past him into the kitchen.

'I'll light the lamp,' she said.

Thomas had woken. He had been listening. He reached out and clutched her wrist.

'He came back, girl! Remember that.'

Light from the lamp spilled into the room, swamping the candle flame. She leaned over and adjusted the wick. The lamp flared higher. She was trembling.

'OK. I suppose Papi's right about you. You didn't have to come back.'

'It's better to be suspicious. Did the Gestapo question you?'

'I was one of the lucky ones. I was taken to that place in the lorry. Our papers were checked. Three were detained, but they set me free. I told them I had a fish stall in the market, that I supplied lobster to the Kommandant, and I was just having my break in the café. One of them recognised me. And I had that bill for the Kommandant! You remember! That was a piece of luck. But there was a horrible man there. He made my flesh creep.'

'They may check back on your papers. You've got to get out quickly.'

'No, I don't think so. I'm sure they were satisfied. Anyway, the gendarmes in Sainte Croix all know me. I've been on the market stall for ages.'

'But some people know I'm here, at *Le Tamaris*. You'll both be in danger. It isn't safe. You'll have to come with me to Château-Le-Vigny. Paul gave me a message today. They're going to get you out in the next moon. I'm sure they'll let you take Thomas too. Believe me, it's the best thing!'

He talked desperately, seeing the puzzled face of the old man, grasping for words out of his darkness, her set face.

'Will you be coming too?' she said.

'No. I have to stay. I've a job to do. That's why I came here.'

'Papi doesn't want to leave. I have already told him I'll only be away a little while. He and Jacques have to keep the farm safe. He'll be OK. I'll need a place, you see, to broadcast my messages. I've explained it all.'

She looked up at him.

'I thought, you see, that they might let me be your radio operator. I could work with you.'

'Yes, I guess...'

They would never let him work with her again. And she would never be allowed back in the area. But he had to say anything to get her away.

'You must understand there's so much to arrange! The care of the farm, important financial matters. Until we get back. I can't just leave straight away.'

She looked across at Thomas. He was staring sightlessly into the dark, straining to hear. Pierre could see she was uncertain, now the thing she had wanted for so long was close.

'You must both come to Château-Le-Vigny. Now. Both of you.'

'No! *Le Tamaris* is all we have. We've talked about it. It's important that this place stays safe, for me to come back to. What's the point of fighting if you come back to nothing?'

She crossed the end of the table and stood behind the old man, putting her face against his.

'As soon as I've had another message from London,' Pierre said, 'you must be ready.'

She was watching him with those fierce eyes, standing there in an old canvas smock several sizes too large, those ridiculous trousers, her arm around Thomas's shoulders. She left the table abruptly and moved over to the range.

'Have you eaten?'

'Yes! Kind of. I'm afraid I burned the stew.'

'Coffee! I'll make more coffee!'

She opened the fire and the red light swam around the walls. He stood up and moved over to where she was grinding more coffee.

'Rebecca...'

The old man had fallen asleep again. Squatting by the low cupboard, she lifted out the bowls.

'Are you OK? I mean, did they hurt you?'

She shook her head.

'No! It was not the *Miliciens*, thank God.'

'You have to understand. You are *both* in real danger. You must leave!'

The coffee pot began to boil. That bitter smell of acorns.

'Rebecca, I've got to go tonight. Being here would mean the death penalty for you both. Paul and the group will look after you. Get you to the pick up on time.'

She was spilling more water. Her hand dabbed ineffectually as it ran down between iron roses on the range, trickling like tears, pooling on the floor. He put his hand on her arm.

There was a crash in the yard. They both jumped. Grabbing the lamp, he dashed out of the door. Nothing but a wall of black, a moth blundering towards the light. A shape struggling up from the ground, swearing.

He leaned against the doorway, feeling sick.

Rebecca beside him. 'What is it?'

'It's OK. It's Genier, the damned fool.'

She left his side and ran into the dark, her clogs splintering ice on the puddles. She dragged Genier into the light. He was clutching his stomach.

'That damned pump! I went straight into it in the dark. And I must have lost kilos bicycling here so fast.'

'Something urgent?'

'Of course. You don't think I'd work myself to a shadow getting here if it wasn't urgent! I have better ways of spending my time!'

'Get on with it!'

Rebecca led him through the doorway into the kitchen. Thomas had woken. They all shook hands. Genier accepted a glass of *marc*.

'Cheers! Now I'm beginning to thaw out. This is good *marc*, Thomas. Very good. It was the *message personnel*, Maurice! A drop tonight! I could hardly believe it myself, but there it was. Such a singularly appropriate quotation — *Qui vit sans tabac n'est pas digne de vivre.* Indeed! That reminds me, you haven't any more of those wonderful English cigarettes?'

Genier emptied the glass.

'Genier, we have to get going!'

'We were wondering if Mademoiselle Rebecca might lend us the *gazo* for the night. There will be a large number of canisters to transport, with any luck! And we have nothing but two carts and two *bidets anciens*, all we have left since the Boches came to the village and requisitioned the heavy horses.'

'Of course. We don't mind, do we, Papi?'

The old man shook his head, puzzled by the noise, the air of excitement.

'Are you going tonight, my girl?'

'No, Papi. But Jean has to go with M. Genier. Can they borrow the *gazo*?'

The old man nodded.

'I may not be back until it's time for you,' Pierre said. 'Once we have done the drop, I'll have to find a new safe place. Genier will bring back the *gazo* and then he can collect his bicycle.'

'My bicycle is now irretrievably broken, Maurice. I was hoping that you would bring its remains home in the back of the *gazo*, give it a decent burial perhaps.'

'Rubbish! Bicycles are too useful. You can bring tools to mend it when you come back tomorrow.'

Rebecca had gone up to his room and returned, carrying his fibre suitcase.

'All your things are in here,' she said. 'Now there's no need for you to come back. You said it isn't safe.'

'No. I will come back. To fetch you. It will be soon. Maybe in one or two days. You have to come then. There won't be another chance.'

He didn't want to be more precise in front of Genier. It was supposed to be secret, this Lysander pick up.

'Genier,' he said. 'I want to say goodbye to Thomas. Could you go and get the *gazo*? I've parked it in the copse on the right-hand side in the lane to Davide's place.'

He shook hands with Thomas. He remembered he had some chocolate in the side pocket of his suitcase, and he gave it to the old man. Thomas raised himself in his chair. Taking Pierre by the shoulders, he kissed him on both cheeks.

'You are always welcome!' Thomas said.

He stood with Rebecca in the doorway, awkwardly like strangers. It was bitterly cold, the stars very bright. Frost in the air. A three-quarter moon. A good night for a drop.

She had left the lamp inside. Pierre couldn't see her face.

'I want to come to the drop. Please!'

'You can't. It's too dangerous. Anyway, you don't know the drill. Maybe next time.'

'There may not be a next time. You know that.'

'I'll send a message as soon as I know more about Château-Le-Vigny,' he said. 'You must be ready to go any time.'

'Yes.'

'You're sure about everything?'

'Yes.'

'Rebecca, I have to keep away from here. It isn't safe for you. But you *do* have to come with me next time.'

'I know.'

He heard the *gazo* returning.

He began to walk away. Then he turned back into the doorway, where she stood in the dim light.

Her hair, a scent of rosemary; the taste of salt on her mouth.

Genier came into the yard, the *gazo* misfiring, making a racket. She slipped away from him and into the house. Genier stayed in the cab and Pierre climbed in beside him, carrying his suitcase. Genier said nothing all the way. He was a good friend, the fool.

10

Rebecca stood in the doorway for a long time, looking out at the moonlit yard, the ducks and geese sharp-shadowed against the cobbles. It must be cold but she didn't feel it. She touched her mouth where he had kissed her.

He should have let her go with him. She could be useful. What if the *gazo* broke down and they were stranded? It was making a terrible noise. She knew how to fix it. She didn't let herself think about the kiss. Not too much. Just enough to know. Now he had kissed her, there was real danger. She could deal with the other kind, but this was something else, forbidden territory. She knew Papi would be angry if he knew, even though she was a woman, and could do as she liked. But this wasn't some mild flirtation. She'd had those, when she was younger. The lad in Evreux who was killed in the bombings. A long time ago. On that terrible day when so much was lost.

This was serious. She was on fire. Longing to burst out, longing to be free. She had been like one of the ducks in winter, trapped in ice, swimming round and round to keep a tiny space clear, so that she could survive.

Perhaps she was just vulnerable on her own here. Mostly the only people she saw were on market days, and Paul. She knew Paul liked her, but this was different. The little things which had a kind of glow about them, the bowl she'd put in front of him with his coffee. She had tried to show him how she'd felt. But he was shut down, anxious not to cross boundaries, not to impose. So serious. Now, he was the one who had crossed the line.

She shut the door and went back in the kitchen. As ever Papi seemed to be asleep.

'You want to watch it, girl! You'll get yourself in trouble,' he said as she walked past. She started to wash the dishes in the sink, looking through the window into the night.

'Time he was leaving, Rebecca,' he said. 'I may not be able to see, but I can feel what's going on.'

'Feel what, Papi?'

'You know, lass. One day he'll make a bad decision, because of you.'

'I know.' She dried the dishes with the old cloth. 'Anyway, he's left.'

She helped Papi to bed, and then went to her room. She wouldn't sleep till the *gazo* came back.

She switched on the light, and there on her bed was a package, roughly wrapped. For a moment, she thought it was from him, but then she saw the scrawled hand on a piece of paper underneath. Papi could still write, despite his blindness.

Happy birthday, my dear grandchild. You are precious to me. I want you to have this.

Her birthday today! Her twentieth. She hadn't even thought of it. But then Papi had never forgotten, not since she had come to live with them. Usually, he never came up there. His bed was in the back kitchen, and he had the WC down there. She brought the water to wash, but he always washed himself. He was a proud man.

Inside the wrapping was a ring — her grandmother's engagement ring. The one she always wore. Tiny diamonds and a blue sapphire. It had been kept in the drawer of the old chest in the sitting room. Rebecca imagined him, groping his way across the kitchen, finding the drawer, somehow finding paper and a pen, writing in his shaky hand, sometime in that long day when she had almost been lost. He had fumbled his way up the stairs. Then he had waited, alone, in the dark kitchen. To give her that gift for her twentieth birthday. For a moment, the memory of the day swamped her. The fat man with the lizard tongue.

She slipped the ring on her finger. It fitted. He'd told her once he had sold a half share in a trawler to buy it, that and a record catch off the Îsles de Glénan. In the end it had slipped off

53

Grandmama's finger as she wasted away. He had tried to nurse her alone, his sight already going, until Rebecca came.

***

Genier lay beside Pierre under the hedge, breathing heavily from his second bicycle ride of the night. Old Boutron had lent them two bicycles and told them where they could hide the *gazo* close to the road before the drop, three kilometres from the DZ. They had loaded the bicycles and cycled the last bit at speed. Time was getting short. The bicycles were old, with curved frames and Genier's had a pointed saddle. He complained the whole way.

The others had been waiting anxiously, but there were enough of them to stake out the Dropping Zone if Pierre didn't arrive. They knew the drill.

The old nag was snuffling into her nosebag at the bend in the track. She would have to pull the *plate-forme*, the flat truck, by herself as far as the *gazo*. There were no other horses left. LeFaivre's brother-in-law was holding her head. LeFaivre and Jean-Marc were halfway down the field. He could see the glow of their cigarettes along the corridor of mist. The field was close to the water meadows, and the river damp lay across it like a white slab, so chill it went deep into the bone. Not even swigs of Genier's cognac could keep it out.

Madame LeFaivre had sent out hampers, and good blankets. They made themselves shelters with some of the wood cut by a *charbonnier* at the far end of the field.

Above the plateau of the mist, the three-quarter moon shone down over the river poplars; a clear, frosty sky. Perfect visibility.

Genier belched softly and delved into the hamper for another slice of ham. He wrapped it around his huge fingers and stuffed it into his mouth.

'You're a pig, Albert,' Pierre said. He felt a sudden wave of affection for the fat grocer. One bat-like arm blotted out the stars as Genier swept him up in his own blanket.

'Keep warm! I heard you cough, you young idiot. Those lungs of yours!'

It was good to be there, sharing ham and bread and the searing cognac out of the bottle. He tried not to think about Rebecca. How could he have done such a thing?

'We could have a long wait,' he said, looking up at the moon. 'Another two hours perhaps.'

Genier groaned.

'What am I doing here? Sitting here, on a freezing night in the middle of winter, waiting for an English plane! It's a joke! I never fired a gun before the war, not even to shoot a pigeon for the pot. Now I talk about Brens and plastic explosive, blowing up railway lines as though they were my mother's middle names. It's insane!'

He snorted, and rummaged in the hamper.

'I tell you, I don't believe it myself. It's different for the others ... for Jean-Marc and Robert, and Paul. And what about you? How do you feel about all this? You're young, after all. Too young to be messing about with all this. It's too damn dangerous.'

'I'm old enough.'

'For some of them, it's the best time of their lives. When it's all over, if they survive, they'll be errand-boys and apprentices. Life will be boring. But for now, they are gods. Really something!'

Genier drained his cup. Then he collapsed back into the hedge, with a cracking of branches.

'A quiet stomach and a quiet life. That's all I ask! But I can't help it. I'm forced into such ridiculous behaviour by my hatred of the Boches. Ordinary life is now impossible. I'm a stranger in my own country. But no one will say after the war, Genier, fat grocer, you are a hero of La Résistance? I guarantee they won't. What shit!'

As Pierre walked down, he could just make out Jean-Marc, thin and lanky, lolling against a tree. LeFaivre was stretched out along the roots, snoring, his cigarette, still stuck to his lower lip, spraying sparks into the dark.

'You'll catch yourself alight!'

A hand came up out of the blankets. The glow of the cigarette stub arced across the frozen ground.

'It's about done, anyway. But a man has to keep himself warm, when he should be in bed.'

Pierre told them about the raid. They already knew most of it already.

'And Rebecca? We heard she was taken!' LeFaivre said.

'They let her go, but I'm still worried,' he said. 'Whatever happens, after this drop we must lie low. We've been very lucky so far.'

LeFaivre lit another cigarette. 'My last! They'd better come tonight.'

'It's very grave.' Jean-Marc always spoke in a pedantic voice, like a schoolmaster. Maybe that was what he would become after the war. 'I am becoming more of the opinion of Monsieur Maurice. It is exactly the method of the Gestapo to behave in this way, waiting for the correct moment.'

LeFaivre closed his eyes with a sigh. Tilting his cap forward, he leaned his head back against the tree root.

'LeFaivre, I'm going down to check on the others.'

'OK, Maurice. I'll keep an eye out here!'

Madeleine and Robert were staked out with their torches further down the field. His feet rustled dryly in the frosty grass. Something screamed in the wood. One blanketed shape against the grass. He heard them laughing. He thought about Rebecca again, the impossibility of it all.

He made his way back. Genier looked up at him.

'Those two are making the most of it! Don't tell them off. They don't get much time together! Time is precious, after all.' He pulled out a white handkerchief, trumpeting loudly into it. 'What's the time? Surely it can't be too long. I'm getting a cold. I can feel it coming.'

There was a peculiar grunt far, far out in the pale bell-jar of sky. Pierre stood up.

'Shut up! Listen!'

They could hear it — a succession of low growls which grew until the sky seemed to shake with it. They were all there, even Madeleine and Robert, half-bodies in the mist, torches high. The noise was so loud now it seemed impossible the Germans weren't there already.

The huge sound battering on their eardrums, the black shape coming over them, moonlight washing the perspex dome — unzipping the veil of stars and white mist, a wonderful, obscene sound. Pierre stood with Genier as he held the first torch. The shattering roar went through them. Then parachutes were opening like flowers in the moonlight, falling among them, containers chunking against the iron-hard earth.

The group were all over them before they settled. Tearing at them while they were still half-inflated, straddling the length of the cylinders like hunters before the prey is truly dead. The great black plane roared over them again and Genier, who knew the Morse code, flashed 'OK. OK. OK.' until the torn veil was sewn back again by degrees into silence.

'They wanted to see us!' Genier said proudly. 'He flashed his wings...' He stretched out his arms in the mist, 'So!'

Madeleine was already folding the dark parachutes, the silk rasping through her fingers. The others moved ahead of her through the frozen grass, unhooking the containers. Genier, Robert and Pierre lifted out the canisters — three to each container — and staggered across the field to the *plate-forme* where the horse stood, stamping with cold. The handles cut their frozen hands like wire into cheese, too cold to bleed. One container had fallen on the far side of the hawthorn thicket where there was a ditch. It seemed to take hours to get out. They swore about the sharp spines of hawthorn, the sweat of fear running down the inside of Pierre's smock. After the shattering noise of the Halifax, they were afraid. The Germans must be coming. Soon.

Then it was done. Only swirling funnels of mist to show where they had sunk the containers and the parachutes. As they left, the canopy of mist smoothed again; the sky rang empty as a wine glass. And still they didn't come.

11

Old Besson and LeFaivre added their weight to the horse. The rest lay back against the brushwood piles which hid the canisters. Madeleine and Robert went ahead as an advance guard on the bikes. They waited close beside the *route departmentale*. The *gazo* was hidden behind a haystack. The moon was setting, but they could still see the way clearly, long shadows of poplars along the route. The road was full of potholes. It was not used much by the Germans, who hadn't bothered to repair it. It was an uncomfortable journey in the *gazo*. Pierre kept thinking of the explosive power packed in the canisters.

They hid the cache under the boards at the back of Boutron's barn, a few kilometres from the house. If the cache were found they could always claim they knew nothing, but he didn't seem to care either way about the risks. He was a tiny man, stringy, emaciated, mad with hate against the Schleuhs who had taken his son with the STO and worked him to death in a German factory. There was no one to pass the farm on to now. His wife dead before the war, there was nothing left he cared about.

But he knew how to cook. He had laid on a feast. It was early morning but still dark, the mist thickening before dawn. They would stay there at the isolated farm till after curfew. Boutron was happy, honoured to entertain them.

Here, in his kitchen, under his roof, *La Résistance!* He poured cider, and the fingers which held the best glasses had touched weapons which the British RAF had dropped. What havoc and fire they would spread! He wanted to have a hand in such things himself, even if it were only to fuel revenge with rabbit pie. Enough for the moment.

'Of course,' said Claude, swinging one leg up onto the table and examining his boots carefully; new boots. 'It's all different now. Once we were *resisters de premier heure.* We were alone then. Nobody wanted to know. Not even the British. Now we are useful. The ultimate honour! A British agent to set us on the path to glory!'

LeFaivre stood up, his chair falling backwards onto the brick floor. He unpeeled the cigarette stub from his bottom lip.

'Maurice is one of us. We can trust him,' he said softly.

Claude's small eyes darted around the room.

'How do you know? It's well known in Sainte Croix that Maurice is sleeping with the red-haired bitch from *Le Tamaris.*'

The room went very quiet. Nobody moved except Boutron, still scurrying across the floor with his brown jug, filling glasses.

'You're drunk,' LeFaivre said.

Claude leaned back in the chair. His Adam's apple showed white above his collar. 'Everyone knows that Mademoiselle Rebecca has friends in high places. Friends who enable her to fish in the *Baie* without registering at the port. Without returning there at night as the Luiset brothers are forced to do. She's even allowed to run a *gazo* for her business without permits. Explain that!'

He got to his feet.

'Got to have a piss.'

He brushed past them out of the door.

'Let's just calm down.' LeFaivre said. 'We're all tired. It's been a long night.'

Suddenly, the room was almost empty. Robert, Madeleine, Jean-Marc and LeFaivre had all melted away. Only Genier sat stolidly at the table, sucking slowly on crumbs of rabbit pie. Boutron came in through the kitchen door with kindling for the range.

'Where's Claude?' Pierre asked. 'He's been gone a long time.'

Genier looked up. He pulled out his handkerchief and mopped the sweat on his forehead.

'Sleeping it off, I shouldn't wonder. It's hot in here, Boutron. Don't stoke up the range.'

But Boutron went on feeding kindling into the glowing fire.

'We've got to do something about Claude.' Pierre said.

Genier leaned forward, his fat hands spread on the table.

'Were you ever in the mountains?'

'Never, not in France anyway.'

'Ah, you have missed something. I went once, to St Etienne, with my wife, and the boy when he was young. Before the war. Sometimes, I long to be there again. You can't imagine the peace! And there is something about high places. Perhaps we should go there, eh, Maurice? They say the *maquis* rule the mountains in the west. That the Schleuhs can't defeat them. How about that!'

Pierre got up.

'It's time we left, Genier. It's after curfew. You've got to return the *gazo*.'

He groaned. 'Shit! I'd forgotten all about it. But I must have some sleep. I'm worn out.'

'I want that *gazo* out of here today, Genier. We will have to lie low for a while. Claude doesn't know where we have hidden the stuff? I don't trust him.'

'It wouldn't take much intelligence to guess it might be in Boutron's barn. Claude's nobody's fool. However, I don't think you need lose any sleep about it.'

LeFaivre came back into the room, half-carrying a slight figure. It was Paul. He was bleeding badly.

'I'm sorry, Maurice.' Paul's voice was faint. 'There was a road block. I turned round. They shot at me.'

Pierre peeled back his thin jacket with its too short sleeves. He had taken off his scarf and bound it to stop the bleeding. It looked bad. Pierre picked up the jacket and turned it over. He found the small hole and waggled his finger through it.

'Is there something still in your arm, Paul?'

'Yes, I think so. I'm sorry I couldn't deliver. There may still be a drop this moon, after all. We can't stop it.'

'It's alright, Paul, it's happened already. We knew about it. Don't worry.'

'And Rebecca. Could she be still be picked up?'

'We'll talk about that later. We may need to find a doctor to look at that wound. Did anyone see you come here?'

'No, I just met LeFaivre on the road.'

'I was going home with the cart,' LeFaivre said, a little too quickly.

'What's going on, Pierre? Where are the others?'

He shook his head.

'Don't ask me. You don't have to worry about Durand, by the way. Our friends have taken care of him.'

Pierre remembered Boutron's face as he fed kindling onto the range. He had that feeling again of ranks closed against him, protecting him, as the farmers' wives hoarded butter for his visits, so he wouldn't know they were starving.

LeFaivre's face was grey. 'We were sure he was a collaborator. Now we are all in danger. We've made plans. But you have to move on. It's much riskier for you.'

'Let's get out of here, then,' Pierre said. 'Now.'

Boutron came into the room, a bowl of hot water and a cloth in his hands.

'That boy can't go anywhere!' he said. 'He needs a doctor for that arm. I'll look after him. He's only young. He shouldn't be in this war.'

'I'm old enough!' Paul winced as Boutron dabbed at his arm.

'Keep still! You remind me of my son. He was no older than you. Soon there won't be any young men left.'

He turned to LeFaivre.

'Will you try to send the doctor? Dr Dubois in the village is a good man. He'll keep quiet.'

Pierre turned to Genier.

'Will you take the *gazo* back to *Le Tamaris*? We have to get Rebecca and the old man away — take them to Château-Le-Vigny. They'll know what to do with them there.'

LeFaivre put his hands on Pierre's shoulders.

'No, Maurice! If the Gestapo come to the village, how can *you* hide? If we're caught, it was always Claude's word against ours. But it's different for you. There's important work for you — in other *reseaux*. If you stay, you'll risk all that.'

'OK. I'll go.'

Pierre was driving the *gazo* out of the gate of Boutron's farm when Robert came fast round the corner on a petrolette, and avoided a collision by skidding into the wall. He was in his gendarme's uniform. He picked himself up out of the mud and waved to Pierre to stop.

'They've taken Madame LeFaivre,' he said. 'Claude's wife has been shooting her mouth off this morning. Claude hasn't come home. She's stirring up a hornet's nest.'

'Did you...?'

'They won't find him yet. But they're on their way out here, and they could also be watching Rebecca's place. Someone else must have blabbed.'

Pierre shot out of the farmyard in the *gazo*, the tyres spinning on the cobbles.

12

There was no way round Sainte Croix but Pierre kept to the residential roads and nobody stopped him. He couldn't cross the *Zone Interdit* in the *gazo*. All the patrols would be alerted now. He turned off the road and drove a little way along a track which led into the edge of the beech forest. There he bumped the *gazo* off into the trees. He left it there, thankful he had slung one of Boutron's old bicycles in the back.

On the Michelin map, there was no road or track which headed even remotely near *Le Tamaris* without crossing the Zone. But if he went cross-country at an angle he would hit a farm road on the far side of the Zone, only skirting the edge. Pierre cycled cautiously, only once seeing a German motorcycle going very fast along the road to the south.

The little overgrown track which led into the farmyard at *Le Tamaris* wasn't shown on the map, but he found it at last, not quite where he expected. He pulled up the sign for the farm, pushing it out of sight under the hedge. He hid his bicycle, and pushed on through the undergrowth.

He was worried about the geese making a racket when he came out by the pond, but someone had just put grain down for them and they were busy gobbling. Perhaps things were still OK. He was just about to make a dash for the kitchen door, when Rebecca came out.

Pierre stayed in the shadow, watching her, wary that there might already be danger in the house. The weather had changed with the morning; it was one of those moist, rain-spattered days which smell falsely of spring. The frost had melted fast, the yard gleaming with wet. Rebecca had on her old sabots and a pair of Thomas's trousers, her bright hair bundled into a cloth turban. She was carrying a churn. He saw how thin she was.

She came towards the barn. When she stepped into the shadow, he caught her arm. She turned, startled.

'Mary, Mother of God, don't ever do that again.'

'You look white. What's wrong?'

'A German soldier just came here. Just an ordinary soldier, you know. On a motorbike. He would have found you.'

'What did he want? Was he searching for someone?'

'I don't think so. He wanted to give me this.'

She reached into her pocket and handed him a gilt-edged card.

'It's an invitation. Tonight. To the Kommondant's residence. A party. It will be that SS man, the fat creepy one, he'll be behind it. They like to make a splash when they are hooking in their tarts.'

'What did you say? Did he ask you for an answer?'

'I said "yes". What else could I say? Now I'll have to leave with you. I don't have any choice.'

She looked away from him, into the distance.

'I'll keep it though it makes me sick to touch it. Some time it might be useful. I'll get my own back.'

He put his hand on her arm. She was trembling.

'That's what they do,' she said softly. 'Everyone knows it. The girl from the dress shop. She went. They raped her. Three of them. Those respectable SS officers who do everything by the book. A gilt-edged invitation.'

Pierre swallowed, his mouth dry. He had to get her away.

'I'm sorry, but we have to leave now. We have been put on alert to have you picked up by Lysander. I tried to cancel but Paul was shot on the way to Château-Le-Vigny. We're all in the shit; someone's talked. Madame LeFaivre's been taken. They may be on their way up here. It's a real lash-up.'

She looked at him intently, brown eyes in a pale face.

'Why did you come back? You shouldn't have come back.'

'Get Thomas, and grab some warm things. Be quick. You'll have to leave now. The Germans could be here any time. They'll be looking for me.'

'But Papi isn't here.'

'Where is he, for Chrissake?'

'You know he goes down the lane at midday to meet Jacques. They'll be here any minute.'

'I'll go and get him. We can't wait any longer. There may already be Germans on the road. You've got five minutes to pack.'

'But I...'

'Just go.'

He started off across the yard. In that moment, the air was torn apart by a burst of machine-gun fire. Then another, in the lane. The stuttering noise, so close. She was running beside him.

He caught her to him, covering her mouth before she screamed. He struggled with her through the pond, down the old track. She was a wildcat, her teeth halfway through his thumb. Then she was crying silently, great dry sobs.

They wove through the undergrowth of the track, trying to be quiet. They passed the place where he had hidden the bicycle. Retrieving it would make too much noise.

'I'll go out to the road and see what's happening. Stay here!'

There were voices now, beyond the track's end, some way to the right. In German. He struggled to understand.

'Clear this mess away, you idiot.'

'Are you sure it's him? He looks too old.'

'When you called out to him, did he answer in French? No! He spoke in English. I know some English. It must be him.'

'He's nothing. Just an old man. You made a mistake.'

'I don't agree. Didn't you hear what Jünger said? They are clever, these British agents. They change their appearance all the time.'

Pierre slid back under the winter cover, seeing in his mind the rag doll lying on the road, sightless eyes staring at the sky.

13

Rebecca was waiting on the edge of the ditch. Her eyes settled vacantly on his face, the pupils wide with shock. There was no need to tell her anything.

Pierre pulled the map out of his pocket.

'We need to get to the *maquis*. We can't use the road. Is there a path to the beech forest, to Beauforêt?'

Her finger traced a pattern. Small hands, scars from the boat's winch.

'Yes! Here. The old sheep path. First we go across the field, then here....'

She was so quiet all the way. The sky darkened, rain soaked them. They came back onto the road at last and crossed quickly into the beech forest. Rebecca's hair had fallen out of its turban. She was shivering. He pulled her through the narrow band of scrub and small saplings, into the deeper trees.

It seemed warm there, after the rain. Soon they could no longer see the road. Only the arches of trunks, snips of sky. Pierre stopped to look at the map and she sank to her knees, looking down at the dead leaves. She picked them up in handfuls and let them fall, sobbing quietly, her hair a flare of colour against the dying browns and golds. He thought how conspicuous she was. They would have to do something about her hair.

There were no roads through this part of the wood. Pierre remembered the compass in the lining of his smock. They were travelling roughly south-west through the deepest part of the forest.

He remembered one night they'd had a meeting with Jean, the leader of the *maquis*. Perhaps they were still there, holed up in the forest.

'I don't think we are too far from the camp now. Come on! I'll help you.'

By this time it was getting dark, and Pierre was half-carrying her. She was shivering violently and was very hot. He knew they had to find shelter. The rain had stopped, but a night out in the open in winter would be foolish.

At dusk, he saw an outface of granite which rose up out of the forest floor. A large oak had clenched a hold there, among the beeches. Under the roots someone, a woodsman perhaps, had built a rough shelter. It was sandy and dry inside, dry leaves in the corners. Rebecca lay down, turning her head away.

Pierre turned out his pockets carefully. One Michelin map, one revolver, thank God he had it with him this time. Papers in the name of Jean Vacher, a fob watch. No food. He had given the chocolate to Thomas. But then, matches!

Rebecca was sleeping. Pierre took off his jersey and covered her with it, replacing his smock. She had stopped shivering but she was still hot. Then he heaped some of the dry leaves over her, thinking of the nursery story of *Babes in the Wood* he had read when he was ten, learning English.

He went out into the dim wood. At least he could gather some wood and make a small fire, although it would be dangerous.

He walked some distance in every direction, returning between forays. There was no hut anywhere around. Rebecca still slept, and seemed cooler now. He took some fallen branches, trying to sweep away the tracks they'd made, then made a fire in the entrance to the cave. There was a lot of smoke but at least as it crawled upwards out of the woven branches, it tended to disperse and by now it was quite dark. Pierre wished they had food. He could hear the faint cawing of night rooks, but nothing came down to the forest floor.

Rebecca woke, coughing in the smoke.

'How are you feeling now?' he said.

'I'm alright. Just tired.'

'We may have to sleep here tonight. It's going to get pretty cold and we haven't any food, but I don't want to go on in the dark.'

She nodded.

'We'll have to sleep close together, to keep warm.'

'Yes.'

'Tomorrow we'll go on. Find the *maquis*. Then it'll be OK.'

She looked at him. 'I suppose I'll go to England.'

'If that's what you want.'

'There is nothing to stop me now. Why not?'

'Rebecca...'

'I need to be sure ... was the ambush meant for you?'

'Yes.'

He turned away from her and fed broken sticks into the fire.

'I keep telling myself he was an old man,' she said at last. 'It was a good way to serve his country. He would have wanted that. Now they won't be looking for you anymore.'

Smoke stung his eyes. He stared out of the mouth of the cave.

'I'm sorry.'

His reprieve would be short-lived. As soon as they inspected the body back at HQ, they would know.

14

When he woke, Rebecca was sitting in the entrance to the cave. She had taken his knife and was hacking away at her hair, which lay around her, red and gold. She looked at him over her shoulder; a thin face with her big eyes, and, above, clown's hair, in tufts. She had been crying.

Squatting before him, she began to gather the long strands into the pocket of her smock.

'I'll miss my hair,' she said.

They found a small stream cut into the floor of the forest. Rebecca wanted to wash. She sent Pierre to stand guard on the top of the ravine while she undressed. There was still that sense of a false spring. A warm south-westerly came in spurts under the branches. He could see her white nakedness through the trees.

She came towards him, drying herself on her turban, shivering as she climbed the slope.

'It's winter,' he said. 'Get some clothes on!'

They walked all morning, sometimes crossing *cordons sanitaires*, clearings against fire which were overgrown. Twice Pierre thought he heard dogs faintly in the distance.

He wondered who might be searching for them, whether they would ever find the *maquis*. Then about four o'clock, when the sun was red through the barred trees, they heard voices ahead. Rebecca hid while he crawled forward. About twenty young men were standing around on a flat stretch of path. Some were wearing black berets. They were playing *pétanque*.

He came out cautiously, and found himself staring down the barrels of a couple of brens.

'*Maquis?*'

One of the men nodded, and jerked with his gun.

'Go!'

Pierre lifted his arms above his head. Rebecca was being led out of the trees with a gun at her back.

The others clustered round, staring and talking. Their clothes were threadbare.

'I'm a British agent,' Pierre said. 'We need your help, urgently. I'm a friend of Jean's. He knows me.'

'Jean?'

A young man, almost a boy, pushed his way through.

'Jean? He's not in our group. He's for the FTP. For the Communists! How can the British agent be his friend? We follow de Gaulle here.'

There was a ragged cheer.

'Vive de Gaulle! Vive La France!'

'Yes! But it's true the British have supported him,' Pierre said, trying to sound convincing. 'His cause is also ours.'

'So, you are English. Why do you speak French ... so! *Je suis Anglais* ... I don't believe you! I think you are a spy!' He came close to Pierre. 'Anyway, we know Jean's been taken! The Boches caught him on the road this morning with his lieutenant. Perhaps you knew that already!'

'No, I didn't know.'

'There are many traitors about.' He looked at Pierre coldly. 'Two days ago, our leader, Armand Luiset, was taken in a raid.'

'Armand was also my friend. His brother Paul is my courier. I'm Maurice.'

'Maurice, who ran away from the café in the square in Sainte Croix before the raid?'

'I thought the young men in the café were behaving recklessly. I preferred to get away as quickly as possible. In England we're trained to be inconspicuous. We don't wear our colours for all to see. That's why we're rarely caught.' Pierre felt his anger rise. 'I insist, as an accredited representative of the British Government, that you give me proper help and assistance. I have a mission to complete, of the greatest importance to the war effort. My assistant and I are vital keys to the establishment of a Second Front. We work closely with the French Government-in-Exile.' He paused and looked around at them. 'I can assure you, your assistance will not go unrewarded. If I can get to England, I will arrange for a drop of arms and supplies, even boots!'

There was a brief discussion. Pierre thought this young man would make a good leader, if he survived.

'Very well, we'll help you.'

'Thank you. I'm very grateful.'

They led them away from the path on the far side, Rebecca white-faced. They were all painfully young, and something about them made Pierre think they hadn't been together long. They didn't all have weapons — just a few Brens. He wondered where they had got them.

After about half an hour walking through the wood, they stopped in a glade. The leader produced greasy lengths of cloth and bound their eyes. Rebecca struggled and spat at them.

'If you're caught and tortured,' one of the men said, 'you might give away our location. Now you can't.'

'The Schleuhs would never make me say anything, you fool,' she flashed back.

When they pulled off the blindfolds, it was dark again.

Rebecca was standing beside him, rubbing her eyes. Pierre thought, in a moment of tenderness, like a child who had just woken up.

He looked around. They were in a natural hollow, part of the granite escarpment. Pierre thought they could follow it back, if they had to, and find their way to the shelter. He was pretty sure it was part of the same ridge. A good place to choose. Birch, oak and beech saplings sprang out of the floor of the forest and tangled above. There was plenty of room for a camp, but *maquisards* were hidden from the air.

There was a stink of uncovered latrines, a stale smell of unwashed blankets, old clothes. In summer it would be worse.

The *maquisards* seemed oblivious. Perhaps they would be too, Pierre thought, if they stayed long enough. The group seemed anxious to make up for blindfolding them. The leader shouted for hot coffee and bread, and brought it to them himself, perching on the rock beside them while they ate. Rebecca was still very pale. She refused the bread.

It was real coffee and very good. Again, like the Brens, Pierre wondered where it had come from.

'I'm Philippe. We have only been in the woods for six months,' the leader said. 'The same for most of us. We just came to escape the STO. The village nearby supports us, but it's risky for them.'

Pierre nodded, chewing slowly on his bread, dipping it in his coffee to make it more palatable.

'Armand formed us into a group,' he went on. 'He's a lieutenant in the FFI. Did you know that? He's running several groups in the woods around Sainte Croix. He's a great leader. I'm afraid they will torture him in Caen.' He looked at Pierre. 'What do you think?'

Pierre swallowed a mouthful of bread.

'Yes, I'm afraid they will,' he said at last. 'But there's a chance they may not find out about the FFI.'

'Many people knew that Armand was with the Free French. I'm not a fool. I've seen so many deaths already,' he paused. 'The two Marcels, Marcel Rivat and Marcel Frey, my best friends at school. We were always friends. We'd play cards behind the back desk, take our punishments together, afterwards compare the weals on our hands, and on our backsides! First they came for Marcel Rivat, he was apprenticed at the forge. That man was so strong he could crack your arm! I know. He did it to me. But he wouldn't go. First they tried to persuade him. *It's your patriotic duty, Marcel. You can send money back to the old people. You will be helping the war effort.* Blah! Blah! War effort!' He spat into the fire. 'They took him, two men on each side, because he was so strong. Marched him out of the forge. Then he broke free! Ran down the street, through the queue at the baker's. He ran about fifty metres, in his leather apron, flap, flap! Then they shot him. They didn't care, the filthy Boches!'

'I'm sorry!'

'He was a fine man, Marcel. He used to run in the sports every year. And throw! You should have seen him. There was never any one like him in the village.'

'What happened to the rest of you?'

'We had a meeting that night. All of us. Everyone was angry, and we knew it would be us next. We decided we'd come up into these woods and make a camp — Marcel Frey and I. The others followed. The youngest here's only fifteen, but he is a genius with the Bren. That's how we got started. We knew about this place. We used to come here as boys and sleep out, you know how youngsters do, and everything was planned. We would all bring a cooking pot, cups and some food, a knife and fork each, and blankets. We thought it all out.'

'But before we could get away, they came for Mika Frey — that's what we used to call him to distinguish him from the other Marcel. He was getting a basket of eggs for us, from his father's chickens. He hid in the loft above the chicken house when he saw them arrive, but the officer came into the coop, climbed the ladder and found him. They took him away. He's not very strong, Mika. He had bad lungs every winter, and he couldn't fight. But now he's dead. They told his mother he tried to escape from the camp. They shot him on the wire.'

It was getting cold. A young boy came to Rebecca and wrapped a blanket round her shoulders. Philippe got to his feet and shouted. A shambling figure came through the camp, carrying a large pot. A tall, hunched creature with a long beard. Clothes hung from him in strips, odd bits of sacking wound round here and there for decency. Someone, one of the young boys, came behind him with a light. The boy cleared a space in front of them with his foot, setting the acetylene lamp in the centre. The figure bent down, placing the cooking pot in the bright disc of light. Rebecca gasped. He had no nose — just a strange leprous cavity in a young face; below, a beard stained with mucus.

'This is Boris,' said Philippe. 'We don't know his real name. He's dumb, but the best cook in the world. Isn't that true, Boris?'

The figure grunted. An appetising smell was coming from the cooking pot. Rebecca came forward, moving into the circle of lamplight, putting her hand on his arm.

'What happened to you?' she asked, leaning forward and touching his cheek. A pair of blue eyes looked back at her, startling blue in the lamp, but dark with an indescribable emptiness.

'We think he was a Russian prisoner of war, but no one here speaks Russian, so we can't ask, and he can't tell us,' Philippe said. 'Something happened to his tongue too. Anyway, we're looking after him, and he looks after us in return.'

Boris served the food in old tins; a rabbit stew, with herbs. He offered a tin to Rebecca, nodding. She took it and ate a little. Sometimes, he would take a spoonful of stock from the pot, emptying it slowly into the side of his mouth.

When he had gone, leaving the lamp, Rebecca said, 'I've seen others like that. Prisoners from the Russian Front. They're building the Wall. They're less than nothing to the Boches. They work them till they die.'

'Philippe,' Pierre said, 'thank you for your hospitality.' He stood up. 'I give you my word I'll try to help you in return. But we have to get away from here. Rebecca has to get to England to train as a radio operator. As you know it's very dangerous work, but she will come back to France and help us win the war. I have to get her to Château-Le-Vigny for a pick up. We may already be too late, but we must try. We've also got to find another radio operator, so we can find out what's happening.'

Philippe nodded.

'I'll send out some men into the villages to ask questions. By tomorrow, we'll know a lot more. Until then, perhaps it's a good idea for you to get some sleep. We haven't got any tents, but we've built shelters and there's a cave we've dug out under a tree.'

He picked up the lamp and led them over the slope, kicking old cans and clothing out of the way.

A little away from the rest of the camp, there was a dark hole under the roots of a tree. Philippe poked his head inside and shouted.

'Come out! The lady's going to sleep here. You'll have to doss down with the rest of us, worse luck!'

There was a scuffling in the dark. Boris's shaggy head appeared out of the entrance, like a hermit crab out of its shell.

'They don't like him near them, the boys. They say his nose smells — but that's the last thing it does! But they'll have to put up with it for now.'

Boris squinted up at us as he got to his feet.

'Mademoiselle, ici!' Philippe shouted.

Boris nodded, and ambled off, clutching a handful of sacks around his body.

'He doesn't feel the cold, that one,' Philippe grinned.

A young boy, no more than twelve, came running over with a couple of blankets.

'Will you be alright here?' Pierre said. 'I thought it would be better for you to have your own place to sleep,' he said.

She looked up at him.

'Of course. Don't worry about me. Everyone's been very kind.'

She had bent to go into the cave, but then she stood up again. The lamp was on the ground by their feet, the light casting sharp shadows on her face, her eyes dark.

'How could I?' she burst out. 'How could I flirt with you like some ... some *gonzesse*! How could I, when he's lying dead on a slab somewhere!'

She half knelt in the entrance to the cave, and caught hold of the lower half of his legs, hugging them. She was shaking and sobbing. Awkwardly, he bent down and stroked her hair.

Then he wrapped her in the stale blankets, and took her with him under the claws of the tree.

15

Philippe was shaking him. 'Allez!'

It was still dark. Sometime in the night, the frost had crept back. He left Rebecca sleeping. There was a damp patch on the hollow of his shoulder where her head had rested.

'What is it?'

Pierre was bone-tired and cold. He walked over to the last embers of the fire and stirred them with his foot, stretching out his hands.

'Come out of the camp,' Philippe whispered. 'We've got to talk, but I don't want anyone to overhear.'

Pierre followed him up the slope.

'You'll have to do something about these latrines, Philippe. They stink.'

Philippe stopped and waited for Pierre at the far side of a group of trees. Dawn was not far off.

'What is it?'

'René came back last night.'

Pierre nodded. He was the boy who had gone down to Very-Les-Bains.

'And the two others are back, the ones who tried to get over to Château-Le-Vigny.'

'Is it bad?'

'Your *reseau* ... ffft!'Philippe snapped his fingers. 'Most of them taken.'

'Who? Do you know who?'

'No. Sorry. René doesn't know any more. It's a bad place at the moment. He couldn't ask many questions.'

'And Château-Le-Vigny?'

'There are road blocks on every road. Patrols in the woods. It's no good trying to get there. Something's happened. You can't go there.'

Pierre leaned back against one of the young birches. The rooks were flying up from their roosts, cawing wildly, disturbed by the waking din of the camp, the men going off into the trees for a morning shit. He thought about Thomas, staring into blackness, and Madame LeFaivre that day at the farm, when she had given him a parcel of food to take, an arc of grain falling as she fed the geese. Armand probably dead, and Durand's body taking his secrets to a shallow grave. Someone must have talked; perhaps the radio at Château-Le-Vigny had been turned around, the Lysander sucked into a trap.

They could see each other clearly now, in the dawn light.

'I've got to get access to another radio,' Pierre said.

'That's why I wanted to talk to you.'

One of the boys appeared, striding purposefully through the brush, unknotting the string of his trousers. He stopped when he saw us.

'Not here, you filthy salud! Use the pit.'

'I have a friend,' Philippe went on. 'In my home village. Only Henri and I know about him. You know Henri? He's the tall one, growing his hair long.' Pierre nodded. 'It's very dangerous. This friend is a priest. He worked with Armand. In fact, he brought Armand to us.'

'Does he have a radio?'

'No, no. But he'll tell you where to find one. He'll get you away, give you disguises, and papers. He's a genius. And he trusts us! He calls us his lieutenants. I'm proud to be his friend.'

'I would be honoured to meet him.'

He nodded. 'Tonight, I'll take you there. Henri will go first, to a "letter-box" and he'll leave a message, so that our friend will know. Tonight, while the camp sleeps, I'll take you both. You couldn't be in better hands. The Father will solve everything, with God's help.'

When they got back to the camp, Rebecca was awake. She was sitting on the far side of the camp under the trees, peeling potatoes with Boris. He had given her his sheepskin, and she had it draped around her shoulders. She looked up when Pierre came over.

'Hi, there!' she said. They were shy of each other. 'I've had breakfast. Are we going today?'

'No, not today.' He didn't want to say more in front of the others. The boys stood a little way away, cleaning their weapons and watching her.

She spent the day sitting next to Boris. His face shone with joy, and he watched her as the boys had done. When he had a nose he would have been very fine, perhaps Russian, aristocratic. And, when he looked at Rebecca, you could see it there, an old memory of some other time.

'Mademoiselle is a fine cook,' Philippe said. 'It's a shame she has to leave.'

Pierre thought of the flat, doughy bread she made at *Le Tamaris* and which she hated baking so much. Yet she was very suited to this gypsy existence. Looking at her across the clearing, kneeling on someone's coat (they even put their coats down for her), washing plates in an old tin bath, her short hair sticking out of the turban at all angles, mud on her chin, laughing across at him, the memory of the night between them, awkward, he had that feeling again of going over a hump-backed bridge very fast. But perhaps there was nothing, only the abyss, on the other side.

In the night, they woke them both. Outside, in windless, black ice, Henri waited on the edge of the camp. Philippe brought them thin soup with a slice of potato. There was no moon yet. Henri led them down a sloping path away from the camp. Rebecca was shivering. Pierre wrapped one arm around her as they walked, and rubbed her thin hands against his cheek. He thought he would like to see her fat and warm, protected. He longed for warm clothes, for a woollen jersey, thick boots, a great fire.

They walked for over an hour, getting a little warmer. Then they were in open ground — a small valley with a stream, bordered by young poplars. The moon had risen. Pierre could see a church, a huddle of buildings, a road.

Henri left them, and they followed Philippe across the pasture between the forest and the village. The path was rutted into frozen ridges, firm enough for easy walking. There was a farm on the edge of the village, with the wall of a barn abutting the path; a strong smell of cattle, frozen churned-up patches of ground, hoof marks by the gate. Philippe told them to wait by the wall. It was very clear now, with a full moon. He pointed ahead to where they could see the square, lit sharply by moonlight, the silhouette of a church.

They were very cold by the time he came back. All the time Pierre watched the empty space of the square, three sharp lines of lime trees in the rising moon, the bisecting shadow of the war memorial. He didn't see Philippe at all until he was beside them. He was very good.

He took them along the edge of the square, through a gate on the far side. They slipped through into a large, overgrown garden, full of lumps of stone which must have fallen from the house at some time.

'You'll be OK now,' Philippe whispered.

They embraced.

'Philippe, thank you! I'll send boots. Food and weapons! I promise.'

'You'd better! We'll be waiting. Just hurry up with the boots or we will finish up toeless, like Boris!' He hugged them again. 'Merde! Bon route!'

A door opened. They were hustled through French windows into the dark. Pierre could smell beeswax, the damp smell of old houses. He heard a match being struck. Then in the flare of the lamp, he saw the face of the priest.

'Maurice?'

'Yes, Father.'

He came forward, and shook hands with Pierre, kissing him on both cheeks. Then he turned to Rebecca, who was slapping her arms against her sides, shivering.

'My child, my poor child.'

He pulled her into the light. Pierre could see her face, unwilling, suspicious. The priest wrapped her in his huge arms, kissing her on both cheeks. He towered over her even though she was a tall girl. Then Rebecca was crying against his shoulder.

'Ma pauvre, ma pauvre! I understand.'

He lifted her up and put her down again, tenderly, in the only chair. Then he flung open the door of the cupboard beside the fireplace, and brought out a bottle.

'We need *marc*!'

In the back room he had rubber stamps and blank cards and hundreds of photographs, one of which he could make fit the bill. He had costumes and hair dyes and make-up. It took all the rest of the night, what he did to them. In a back room with no windows, his red face sweating, bleaching and plucking and shaving, until there was hardly anything left. They were almost unrecognizable. A cluttered room with wigs and glue and bleach; false papers in a dangerous, incriminating heap. Pierre never knew his name. Long after, when he came back to France, he looked for the house. But as a reprisal for some crime, the whole village had been razed to the ground.

Finally, he brought out two costumes. A monk's habit, and a black robe for Rebecca, with the white headdress of a Sister of Mercy. With her shaved head and thin, holy face, she looked the part to perfection.

'You will be safe in these disguises,' he said. 'The Germans are still trying to be *très correcte*, especially with the Catholic Church. After all,' he paused and went on sadly, 'our Mother Church seems to condone collaboration. Many bishops have spoken out to say that it is unlawful to disobey the Maréchal. I grieve for Mother Church, and for all our sins.'

Each of them was given a small, battered attaché case with well-used prayer books, a rosary, old letters, suitable underclothing, a religious book or two. Other papers and documents were stored away in the priest's house against their return, or if they did not, they might serve someone else. They had new cartes d'identités and new ration books. Everything was prepared.

It was before dawn on the next morning when they left the priest's house. He kissed them again. He held Rebecca in his arms for a few moments. Then he turned out the lamp and opened the door into the garden. There was something about Rebecca, in her black clothes, with a wooden rosary, with her hair shaved back under the white cap. Some quiet acceptance. It made him sad.

They had been given papers and instructions which would enable them to travel to the convent at Les-Anges, where Marie Gillet (Soeur Dominique) was to enter the novitiate. Her priest (Pierre) was escorting her, and then he would travel on to Abbey, ten kilometres further on, where there was a *reseau* which had radio contact with London. The Father also provided them with bicycles.

'Father, I don't know how to thank you.'

'It's nothing! God go with you! Take care of the girl. She is very precious.'

A cockerel crowed on a heap of frozen muck. The dogs of the village were awake and barking. They wheeled the two bicycles out from the priest's garden.

'Go quickly,' he said. 'Skirt the village till you reach the *route departmentale*. Over there.' He pointed to a line of trees. 'Keep going steadily south; follow the map.'

They began to push the bicycles along the line of the hedge, feeling the ruts in the frozen ground. Before they came to the right angle of the hedge, they looked back but he had gone.

16

They had missed the pick up at Château-le-Vigny. It was going to be tricky to arrange another. Even when they had access to a radio, there was an absence of good fields. The Germans had recently decreed that any stretches of land which might be used for landings were to be cut with ditches or covered with debris, 'brûlé', useless. The Abbot himself, a burnt-out stick of a man, worked for three weeks to arrange a new pick up. But they would have to cycle a hundred and fifty kilometres. In that waiting time Pierre didn't see Rebecca once. And the day they left, she seemed even quieter, more withdrawn. They spent a night at a farm forty kilometres from the pick up, with an old couple who gave up their bed for Rebecca. Pierre slept in the hayloft. She hardly spoke to him all that day. Maybe she was frightened of coming to England, grieving for Thomas, perhaps regretting what they had shared together.

The next night they met the *reseau* who were organising the pick up. Two agents from their group were returning from London and they were to be the home-bound passengers. They sat up that night in a garage on the edge of a small village, playing cards and listening for the nine o'clock message — the confirmation on the BBC. Rebecca had brought a piece of embroidery with her from the convent. She sat close to the lamp, squinting over it. It wasn't like her to do sewing, if she could avoid it.

It had begun to snow outside. They cycled the last few kilometres, soft snow squeaking under their bicycle wheels. Pierre remembered cycling by moonlight through the lanes near his house in Brittany to go to Midnight Mass on Christmas Eve. The countryside stood out clearly in the moon and they could see well without lights. Rebecca rode beside him, looking about her, almost greedily, as though she would never see France again.

They had about an hour's wait in the snow. The Germans had dug two trenches halfway down the field. Men from the local group had been busy since dark filling them in, packing the earth down. The agent who was organising the pick up said there was just room for landing and take-off without touching the trenches, but just in case, they filled them in anyway. The agent staked out his lights carefully down the far end of the field, right under the trees.

The Lysander came in on time. Pierre wasn't prepared for the feeling it gave him, seeing the little aeroplane swooping over the hedge, and then off again after checking the field. As soon as the plane turned and landed, he grabbed Rebecca's hand. There was no time for proper goodbyes. They ran, their robes streaming behind them in the wind from the propellers, casting huge shadows against the white field. The landing lights cut out and they were in darkness. Two figures jumped from under the wing, the second handing down cases. Pierre hoisted Rebecca onto the footholds in the fuselage and tipped her into the back section, clambering in after her.

He felt for the handle of the perspex hood as he'd been briefed, and pulled it forward. Then they were in the air, leaving the white field behind, its long, dancing shadows.

'Rebecca?' He groped across the seat and pulled her towards him. 'Are you OK? You're crying!'

She caught hold of his hand and guided it towards her head. He felt the bristling of new hair on the front of her scalp with his fingertips. 'I've got to land in England with this terrible hair!'

There was a crackle from the intercom. He found the headphones and put them on, fumbling for the switch.

'OK chaps?' The voice came through from the cockpit. 'Sorry. Êtes-vous comfortable?' Excruciating French.

'Oui, merci. Thanks for everything. Thank you. Thank you.'

'Alleluia! You speak English. There's a flask of coffee with some rum. Under the seat. Oh, and some chocolate.'

'Merci. Thank you.'

'Spot on, old chap. And on the floor, couple of parachutes. Sorry, you'll have to sort them out in the dark, but if I come back to help you, could be tricky, OK?'

'Yes, yes. Thank you.'

'Don't thank me, old boy. All part of the service. And how's the gorgeous girl?'

'She's alright. I think she's alright.'

'Better come off air now. Jerry may be listening. Don't want him on our tail. Can you keep an eye open? Sing out if you see anything. Bye-bye for now. Hang on and enjoy the view.'

He switched off the intercom and leaned back, looking around him at the starry night. France was unrolling below him through the dome, trees, woods, snowy fields, dark scatterings of farms where old men slept and women lay awake listening to the droning of the aeroplane. Hoping for freedom perhaps. Down there were his friends. He didn't know who was still alive. Down there, too, were the Boches. He leaned across to Rebecca and took her hand.

'Let's have some of that chocolate,' he said in her ear. They sat back against the fuel tank, facing the way they had come.

The foaming line of the coast passed beneath them and they were over the sea, heading for England.

17

They were waiting in the rain. One man he recognized from HQ.

'Maurice! It's good to see you again. Welcome back!'

They shook hands. The pilot was climbing out of the Lysander. Rebecca kissed him on both cheeks. They all laughed.

The driver was a FANY. She drove very fast away from the airfield. He wondered where they were; it was still too dark to see. Rebecca was very quiet.

In the dark, he felt her touching his hand.

'He called you Maurice, but we're in England now!'

'It's still my ops. name. Anyway, I haven't been debriefed yet.'

'It's very complicated!' she whispered. 'I hope I will understand everything. I hope I'll be good at it.'

'You will!'

She squeezed his hand.

'They may take me away somewhere else', she whispered. 'We may not see each other again for a while. Tell me your real name! We've been ... together, after all.'

'I'm Pierre!'

'So you really are French?'

'My mother's French. My father was English. It's a long story. I'll tell you some time. When we see each other again! Do you want...?'

The car stopped. His door opened.

'This is your stop, sir. If you would like to come with me.'

'Will she be OK?'

'She'll be fine, sir. It's all arranged.'

No time to say goodbye.

Although it was the middle of the night, the RAF had put on a meal for him. He felt disorientated, sitting in the Mess, speaking English with hesitation, forgetting words. He thought of Rebecca. In a strange country. Alone. Strange food under the glare of the lights. Would she be alright?

He woke up sometime in the late morning in a bare room, and, reaching out, found that she wasn't there. Of course. He lay back. This was the end. This was what it was about. He knew they were going to look after Rebecca, give her a new identity, so she could go back to France. The Major from HQ had explained when he showed him to his room.

'You'll have to forget about her for a while. Sorry, old chap. We have to keep her identity secret, whether we decide to use her or not. It will be dangerous enough. I'm sure you understand. You've done a good job bringing her out. We're so short of operators at the moment. They're very vulnerable in the field, and we have to keep replacing them.'

He thought of all the things he could have said.

His old uniform had been laid out. Someone had polished the buttons. An orderly came in with breakfast. A car was ready to take him to London. He walked down the corridor; noise and laughter from the Mess dining room, the scent of bacon. He glanced in. A long table of officers was being served breakfast. He stood in the entrance hall, waiting for the car. He wondered if she had left already.

London seemed crazy with life, different uniforms everywhere, different faces. The pavements were crowded. He kept expecting to see Germans. The whole capital buzzed with excitement, a feeling of expectancy. But when they stopped at the lights, he saw the faces close to, and then he saw strain and fatigue. There had been a lot of bombings; at one point a whole street of green tarpaulins. In France, they had got hold of the news about the Russian advance and the Anzio landings, but he knew hardly anything about what had been going on in England. All he had gathered so far, from the FANY driver talking to Rebecca in the car, in a mixture of a few words of hesitant English and the FANY's slightly better French, was that nail varnish was impossible to get, and the clothing ration was staying the same for a year.

At HQ he had to go through a lot of questions, with the Colonel sitting in and a debriefing officer making notes. He remembered the first time they had met. That night the phone had rung, out in the hall.

'Lieutenant? So sorry to bother you at home. I wonder if you might come and see me?'

'Who is this?'

'Can't really go into detail, sorry, but it's OK. I've cleared it with your chaps.'

'I'm supposed to be on sick leave.'

'Yes, I know.'

He had been given the name of a hotel in Northumberland Avenue, a time.

'Up to you, old chap. But I would be glad to see you, if you can make it.'

He remembered he had put the phone down and stood staring at the Limoges vase filled with white lilacs on the mahogany table. Weren't they supposed to be unlucky? There was a bead of rain on one of the blossoms. As he watched, it dropped onto the polished surface. He pulled out his handkerchief and wiped it away.

If only the past could be wiped away so easily.

He remembered he had walked from the office up Northumberland Avenue. A spring sky, almond trees coming into blossom. A Great War veteran had been playing a mouth organ with his only hand.

Now, looking back, the whole operation seemed to him like a tragic failure — death; betrayal, a waste of good people. Had they done anything well? Had he? SOE had not been able to make radio contact for a while. Someone from the original group had come on for the first time the day before, but the debriefing officer suspected the radio might have been turned around by the Gestapo. The 'pianist' had made no mention of the break-up of his *reseau*, which was suspicious.

The Colonel was interested in the *maquisards* he had met — Jean Masson, Philippe's Gaullists. Circuits were in disarray, and several 'pianists' had been taken. There had been many arrests.

He asked about Rebecca. All they would tell him was that she would be sent on a training course as soon as possible, but it would depend how she did in the interviews.

At the end of the debrief, he turned to the Colonel.

'I'd like to go back to France as soon as possible, sir. I feel I've failed my friends. I'd like a chance to put things right.'

The Colonel shook his head. 'In this business, I'm afraid there are very few successes. There's rarely a chance to put things right, and it would be dangerous to try.'

They had lunch together. Pierre wondered how he had ever thought him cold, but perhaps the last few months had touched him too. Encouraged by the wine, the strain falling away, he told the Colonel about Rebecca; how he wanted to work with her in France. The Colonel listened, turning the last of the red wine in his glass, while the Baker Street traffic shuddered past in the street.

'I do understand. These things happen all the time. The strain you're under in the field is immense. Relationships are forged in the heat of the moment. Perfectly understandable.'

'It wasn't like that, sir,' Pierre said.

'No, of course not. Didn't mean to devalue. Perfectly understandable'. He paused for a moment. 'The better it is, the worse it is, do you see?'

'But, sir...'

'Strong emotions can get in the way of judgement. That's the thing. Have to be very wary of it. Could put lives at risk. Risky enough, sending chaps off, never coming back. Difficult business, do you see?'

Pierre guessed he was very tired, weary of sending people to their deaths. He had seen it too many times.

They said goodbye. He wished Pierre luck, and shook his hand.

'Glad you're prepared to go back. Sure you'll do a good job. We'll send you on a retraining course. Once you've written your report. New explosives, disruption of communications. That kind of thing. Important to be up to date.'

'For the invasion, sir? If it happens.'

'Yes, we have a specific job in mind.'

On the way out, he saw the same official who had given him his last instructions before he was parachuted into France.

'Good to see you back in once piece, sir! This is the address of a service flat. You can stay for a bit. Rest up while you're writing your report.'

'Is it possible ... I could see Rebecca, the girl I brought with me in the Lysander ... before I go back to France? She's going to train as a radio operator.'

She shook her head.

'I'm sorry, sir! But you know the rules! She'll be staying with a senior officer and his wife somewhere south of London. Then, if she passes the interviews, she'll be sent on the wireless operators' course. She is in the system now. There's nothing I can do. I'm sure you understand.'

Before he left, after signing for his possessions, she caught hold of his arm.

'OK! Maybe we can arrange some leave for you both at the same time, just before you go.'

He remembered she had always been kind.

She hesitated.

'In any case, you had better take a few days' compassionate leave. I'll clear it with the boss. The last we heard, your mother was rather ill.'

'When did you hear that?'

'I'm not sure. It might have been a while. You know how it is. Your stepfather, I believe. They had to put him off.'

'OK, I see. Could I leave my stuff and go straight away?'

'Sorry! Beastly procedure! You'll have to go to the service flat first and check in. They're expecting you. Then just take a few days. Hope the news is good.'

He took a taxi to one of the more anonymous residential parts of London, where people come and go and are not remembered. Then he went to the bank and drew out some of his back pay and bought a large bunch of flowers from a girl by the Underground.

Walking down a street crowded with uniforms in broad daylight, he found he was struggling with irrational fear. Turning a corner, he came on a checkpoint with three bobbies stopping passers-by at random. He walked past, feeling conspicuous, vulnerable. When they didn't even spare him a glance, he realized he was shaking.

'I need some proper leave,' he thought.

He got off the tube, walking the quarter mile to his mother's house. Rain fell relentlessly, and the sky flared yellow. He remembered, with a lurch of familiarity, those roads, the Sunday afternoon feeling of suburbs. England in the rain.

As soon as he came to the gate, he knew something was wrong. Edward's prize topiary, the bell-shaped privet, had a moth-eaten, neglected look. The garden, once well-maintained, was sodden with wet. He walked up the drive. The curtains of the house were closed, the blackout up at the side windows.

Edward, his step-father, opened the door in his dressing gown, unshaven. He stood, clutching the flowers.

'We've been trying to get hold of you for months. They wouldn't tell us anything. She asked for you.'

'Is she...?'

'I'm afraid so.'

'I didn't know until today. I've been away. Under orders. I came as quickly as I could.'

'She wanted to see you. She wouldn't have an English doctor, of course, until it was too late. Always a stubborn woman.'

'I didn't even know she was ill. It was very difficult to get news.'

Pierre remembered the Benedictines working under the floor of the abbey, the D/F vans prowling, the thin face of the friar with a headset banded across his shaven head.

They stood together awkwardly in the entrance hall.

'So sorry! Must be a shock for you,' he said. 'Apologies for the dressing gown. Things have slipped a bit. I'm doing fire watching now. I stopped while your mother was ill, but I started again last night. It keeps me occupied. Annie's down with the bloody flu, so the house is a mess. That's what carried her off, of course.'

'Who, Annie?'

'No, appalling epidemic. Never seen anything like it. Chaps are so dashed low, d'you see. Too much wartime food, not enough sleep. Went down like flies. And your mother — well, she was never strong. She wouldn't take care of herself. Would go back to that bloody dress shop, and down the shelter half the night with this new blitz.'

He squinted at Pierre in the dim light.

'I say, old chap. You look rather peculiar. Damn tactless of me. Come into the kitchen, and we'll get Cook to fix you something. At least she's not off with the flu. Things have gone to pieces a bit in the last few weeks.'

He peered at Pierre again. 'Hope you don't mind my saying, but you look dashed different. I daresay they had good reason for doing that to your hair. Well, at least, you're here now, and you'll be in time for the funeral. We delayed it as long as we could. Damned funny war, this one. Gets a chap in some odd scrapes. Suppose you can't talk about it — hush-hush, eh? Message understood.'

He sighed. 'They told me they thought you'd left the Navy. Very vague about it all. Now you're in uniform again! Well, let's hope we've got you home for a bit now. It'll be nice to have another chap in the house.'

'They gave me a few days' compassionate leave.' Pierre said. 'I'm sorry. I can't stay any longer.'

That night they drank black market whisky. They talked about Pierre's mother; even a little about his father. Pierre had always known he was British, killed in the First World War. It was never talked about. They didn't have time to get married. His mother had gone back to his grandmother's house in Brittany. It was a great disgrace in those days to have an illegitimate child.

'She loved him, you know.' Edward stared into his whisky. 'I always felt second-best.'

It was hard to talk freely. Pierre wanted to confide in him about Rebecca, but he couldn't even tell Edward about his work. That he would be going back to France and there was a chance they wouldn't see each other again.

Several people came to the funeral — Edward's sisters, and the woman who had been his mother's bridge partner. Of course, there was no one from France.

That kind little man, fussing over his bell-shaped privet, bumbling about in his gardening cardigan, had been the only father Pierre had known.

When the will was read, Pierre learned that his mother had left him the house on the Suffolk coast where they had lived when they first came to England. After she met and married Edward, they had kept it for holidays. He hadn't been back there since he joined the Navy. She had also left him his grandmother's small estate in Brittany which, for all he knew, might by now have been broken up, the house destroyed. Pierre had always thought his mother had sold everything after his grandmother died, just to keep them afloat in England.

He had to leave the day after the funeral. He dreaded going back to the service flat, its utility furniture. He was glad to do the report for Baker Street, live in his real world again. He worked for several days, staring out of the dusty windows, sparrows huddled on the tiles by the chimney out of the wind. It seemed a dreary end to everything. There was a café on the street corner. Pierre went there for meals, preferring the company to cooking for himself on the little stove, having to worry about coupons again. The window of the restaurant had been blown in, but there was a sign: *Business as Usual*. Inside, it was pleasantly foggy and warm. When he walked back to his flat at night along the unlit street, searchlights were knitting the sky. The batteries sounded very near. Pierre realised he had never been out at night in a city in France since the war — only on empty roads under the stars.

On the third night, there was an air raid warning. He went down to the shelter under the flats, and sat there until after midnight, half-dozing, with the distant 'crump' of the incendiaries. He couldn't stop dreaming about *Le Tamaris*. He was there in the courtyard, looking for Rebecca. Startled out of sleep, he worried he might have cried out.

It was time to go back to France.

On the refresher course, the air was full of talk about the Second Front. The 'action' *reseau* had been trained for just such a moment. It wouldn't be long now. It was good to feel alive again.

18

He was due to drop into France at the end of the month, when the moon was right. In the meantime, after he had finished the course, he reported back to HQ.

The kindly woman who had helped him before greeted him in the foyer.

'Good news! You've got a few days' proper leave due!' She took his arm. 'I'm afraid you'll have to ring in every day for checks, but in the meantime...' She handed him a slip of paper. 'Her number. I remembered my promise. Strictly against the rules!'

'It's Pierre! Pierre from France!'

'Jean?'

'Yes, Jean. Maurice.' It all seemed so long ago.

'Are you OK, Pierre?'

'I'm OK,' he said. 'Really OK. Just off on leave. Going down to my mother's house in Suffolk. You know, a break before...' he hesitated. 'I wondered ... if you felt like coming, and you didn't have, you know, any other plans...'

'Hang on! I need to speak to someone here,' she said.

He waited, feeding pennies into the telephone. A woman knocked repeatedly on the window of the box.

Rebecca came back to the phone. 'Sorry I was so long. I had to ask. It's OK. I can come. I didn't say who it was. It's against the rules, isn't it? But I am free to go away on leave. They can't stop me!'

'That's wonderful. We could meet near Liverpool Street. You need to take a taxi. It's a Lyons Corner House. Just ask.'

'I think I can find my way! When?'

'Tomorrow? Midday?'

He was overcome with giddiness, resting his head against the cool glass for a moment to catch his breath.

The woman was still knocking, her furious face inches from his own.

He opened the door of the box. 'I say! I'm most terribly sorry. I forgot you were there!'

The woman pushed past him, muttering.

'She'll 'ave had it by now, I shouldn't wonder!'

In the Lyons Corner House, the only chair free was at a table where an old man was sleeping, a tin hat beside him. There were a lot of Americans, arms round each other's shoulders, making a racket. Pierre ordered a sandwich and coffee, knowing it would probably be terrible. A girl came through the steamy swing doors in a FANY uniform, a bag over her arm. He watched her thread her way through the crowded tables. She wasn't so thin, and her hair had grown a little. He stood up, just as the waitress came back with the grey sandwich.

The old man woke with a start.

'I do beg your pardon! Been on duty all night.' Then he saw Rebecca. 'My dear young lady, do take my chair.'

A stockbroker's voice, despite his shabby raincoat.

'Thank you! You are very kind!' She spoke in English, a lilting French accent.

Pierre grabbed hold of Rebecca's elbow, steering her into the chair.

'Have you brought a case?' He was suddenly afraid she might have changed her mind.

'Yes. I was early. I went to the station first and left it at the Luggage Office.'

She said the words in English — carefully. They both laughed.

'Let's go now ... unless you want something to eat.'

The American sergeant at the next table tipped his chair back.

'Say, honey. Can I borrow the salt pot?' She ignored him. Pierre passed it over without a word.

'Gee, thanks, honey.' He winked at her. 'Say, do you only drive officers? How about you drive me sometime?'

Pierre left money on the table for the waitress, and they left.

The train was crowded, packed with troops on short leave, grabbing a few hours. At the level crossings, queues of military vehicles. Pierre woke once when the train stopped, hissing to itself. The large station signs had been taken down, and he had no idea where they were. Leaving Rebecca sleeping, he clambered over the bodies onto the platform. A guard was trundling past with cases on a trolley.

'Three more stops! It'll take a bit of time, sir. Troop movements on the line. Don't tell Jerry!'

When they got to Ipswich, they had to wait ages for a connection. It was cold and only a WVS stall serving coffee at that time of night. Pierre telephoned Mrs Swift, the caretaker who looked after the cottage.

'Don't you worry! I'll make up the fires.' Hearing the Suffolk dialect again brought back a flood of memories, unexpected. It had been a safe place when he was young, safe for him and his mother fleeing from the prejudices of her own family. Could it be a safe place again, just for a little while?

'Hello! Are you still there?'

'Yes, Mrs Swift. I'm still here!'

'We were so sorry about your mother. We sent flowers. What a terrible tragedy. Just when you've come back from the war.'

'Thank you.'

'My nephew Bob, you remember him? He'll come down to Saxmundham with the village taxi. There's two of you, you say? I've aired the beds in both rooms. We'll be glad to see you back. It's bin a while. You always loved the cottage when you were a nipper.'

The station was crammed with uniformed personnel from the bases, coming back off leave. Bob was surrounded by Americans, trying to bribe him for a lift. In the end they took two of them along with them, dropping them off on their way. The taxi was filled with the scent of peppermint gum. One of the

Americans told them he was making a tour of English churches on his leave. He was on bombers.

Bob dropped them at the end of the lane. The cottage was just outside the village, down an unmade track a hundred yards from the sea. Pierre's mother had fallen in love with it because it was so typically English. She had always felt safe in England.

They listened to the whine of the taxi driving away. Pierre could hear the marsh mud popping, and the swish of the tide. The rain had cleared. It was not quite dark, a half moon rising, blue prismatic cones of searchlights along the coast sweeping and joining over the sea. The feathery tamarisk which grew all along this coast cast shadows in the moonlight.

There was no light in the cottage, and Mrs Swift had long gone. Pierre felt for the key under the thatch, where it always was. They stood for a moment in the porch, breathing the damp smell of brick and newly lit fires, the aroma of stew left in the oven.

Rebecca leaned her head against his shoulder. She had taken off her cap. He was overwhelmed by the scent of her. He left the cases and pulled her inside. Moonlight filtered through the window. It was easy to see.

He carried her up to his room with its childhood bed. She was heavy in his arms, and quiet.

He opened the window under the thatch. The night sounds came flooding in, the cool, half-winter air, the turning of the sea. He was shy of her and glad he couldn't see her face. They had been a long time away.

He found the zip on her skirt and all the other complicated things, undressing her slowly. She murmured something in French. The whole world was at his fingertips — silk and wet, with that underhum of warmth, the skin's life. He wanted to show her, tenderly, how precious she had become. He yearned to tell her everything. When they had made love that time before, he had held back, not wanting to risk everything in those uncertain times. But this time there was no holding back. They both felt it — the overwhelming need to be together so completely.

She whispered 'Stay! Stay!' And the sweet flood swept them both away.

Such fools.

19

His dream of walking by the sea with Rebecca was cut short at the checkpoint just outside the village. Only their special passes stopped them from ending up in the police station. Instead, they walked in the rain along the marsh, as close to the sea as they could get behind the shore barriers, the first pink pearls of tamarisk flowering in the dunes. They lay together on the damp sand, looking out at the barbed wire fortifications, planning their future. They would be in France together after the war. They would have three children, chickens and geese. Pierre would fish the boat every day.

In the evenings, she beat him at mahjong. Later, he played Chopin's *Études* for her on the holiday piano, while she fell asleep before the fire. They went early to bed. He hardly slept, next to her in a single bed, looking out at the bright stars, listening to the sea.

One morning, the village bobby walked up the path to check on them. He was suspicious of Rebecca, because she was that ugly thing, an alien. Baker Street had given her papers to cover her stay in England, but Pierre knew they would be in trouble if they were hauled up before the authorities. SOE would be furious; after all, they had broken the rules. But in the end, mollified perhaps by real coffee, he left them alone.

That night they found a toad on the path at dusk. Rebecca brought it in and put it in the sink. She wanted Pierre to go out after blackout and find worms. In the end they set it free, taking it into the dark garden, and watching it hop away along the path. They stood under the thatch by the back door, watching the searchlights switching on, arguing which was their light just outside the village. Pierre thought they could have been happy there, in England, as if they belonged.

On the last afternoon, before catching the train, they took a road which led westwards out of the village. It was Breckland weather. They were both tired; sated with feeling, living too much with the shadow of parting. Knowing this was all they had, he almost wanted it to end. Yet, when it did, he would have given anything to have lived it all again.

There was a small pine wood on the brow of the hill, and a sandy footpath leading down towards an inland marsh. The reeds were bleached white after the winter, and stood above the height of a man. Pierre remembered when he was young hearing that a wildfowler had been lost in the marsh, his body never recovered. The story had frightened him when he was a child. As they walked, they heard the bittern booming over the reeds, the cry of a lost soul, waiting to rise again.

They swung around to face the sea, still shrouded in mist. Pierre was uneasy, knowing there were mines close to the shore. They left the reedbeds, and found an island in a sea of reeds, a small promontory, with heather pines on its summit. A heron flapped up in front of them with a 'crark' and made off towards the marsh. The cry of the bittern throbbed again through the mist; otherwise, no sound. Pierre took off his greatcoat and threw it down on the heather — he was in Army uniform, having just been transferred to the General List.

He turned to Rebecca and caught a look of desolation passing across her face. So even lovers hide from one other. She put her arms round his neck. There were clouds reflected in her eyes. Her face was quite still. She hardly moved her body against him, looking at him with that stillness which always unnerved him.

They caught a crowded train to Ipswich. Rebecca was in her FANY uniform. They waited an hour for a connection to London, sitting in the refreshment room with cups of ersatz coffee and a Spam roll. Now she was back in uniform, he saw in her face that passionate dedication he had seen before. It disturbed him, as it had that night in the priest's house. The face that saints have, perhaps, when they are bent on their own destruction.

Rebecca had been given orders to report that evening to London HQ. He left his bag at the Left Luggage Office at Liverpool Street, and together they found their way through the dim light to the Underground. Children were asleep on the platforms, arms thrown trustingly across the demarcation line. A stench of unwashed bodies. One small boy had lost his model London bus. It had rolled to the edge of the platform while he slept. Rebecca bent to pick it up, and gave it to his mother.

'Thanks!' The woman pushed a strand of hair into a net. 'I must look a sight!' They smiled at each other. 'Good luck to you both!' she called, as they walked away down the platform.

When they got to Baker Street station, Pierre stood with Rebecca in the blackout, listening to a violinist playing somewhere in the tunnel. He held her for a few seconds, her cold cheek pressed to his face. Then she was gone.

20

Had Rebecca gone before him to that country house off the Great North Road? As he waited for the weather to clear over France, he thought of the corners she might have sat in, and wondered if she had walked in the garden. A long time after, he found out she had taken quite a different route, and in the end he understood why.

A group of agents were waiting to go. Pierre was to be landed by Lysander somewhere south-west of Paris, accompanied by a W/T operator. He would work alongside an established 'action' *reseau*, specialising in the cutting of communications. He had been given two sets of messages — one for railway targets and one for a bridge carrying military traffic over a main road. In sequence, those messages would tell him first to prepare himself for D-Day, then that D-Day had arrived. After that, it was all systems 'go'. He had a new identity, new papers.

He had already met his 'pianist', 'Bernard', a young lad who reminded him of Philippe. He told him he had spent seven months in France working for a *reseau* in the south, but he had to get out quickly. They were to be the outward-bound cargo for a pick up of returning passengers from France.

It was spring now in the gardens of the country house; saffron crocus and daffodils clumped in untended grassy corners; even a vegetable plot to feed the house. Last time he had been there it had been autumn. Then he had not met Rebecca. It was different now.

They had a day to wait. They played table tennis, and Pierre walked alone in the grounds, killing time. On the second night, the cloud cover cleared and they took off in the Lysander. There was some flak this time, bursting with slow scarlet beauty below them. The Lysander caught the blast, rocking violently. Bernard was very sick.

Not long after, they spotted the 'L' of the lights in a small clearing between dense thickets of trees. The pilot dropped steeply to circle just above the woods, checking the lights. Then, with a swoop which left his stomach behind, and retching from Bernard, they were down. Pierre pulled back the dome. After the hot, sick smell in the cockpit and the stink of petrol, the sharp night air rushed in. Bernard was handing down his precious R/T set and their own cases, while Pierre stowed the luggage of the incoming passengers.

The Lysander's engine was still running, making a racket. Pierre jumped down and helped the woman passenger to clamber in. She smelt good, French perfume you could still get hold of, if you were clever. He thought of Rebecca, her scent of rosemary. He had a sudden vivid vision of her bending over a W/T set, her headphones clamped across her head, tapping into the night. Then the little dragonfly plane was buzzing up into the sky, waggling its wings in farewell.

They slept that night on a farm some twenty kilometres from the field, and the next day cycled twenty more to a small château on the edge of a wood, which, they had been told, would be safe for 'skeds'. Several members of a local *reseau* had been arrested a few months before and had been taken to the camps. It was a sobering thought. Everyone was being extra careful. Now the 'pianist' in the next group, where they had always sent their messages, had been arrested too. It was the riskiest job. In fact, it was getting more dangerous for everyone. The Boches were jumpy, and there were arrests every day.

There was an old couple in the little château, racketing around in decayed splendour, rooms full of dust and no carpets because the Boches had taken them, spaces on the wall where the pictures had hung, the old people left there only because they had no labour value, and were too frail to move. The house could have been requisitioned, but the great château by the lake nearby had been a more tempting prospect, the owner a willing collaborator, as long as her precious Persian carpets could be stored in the cellar.

Pierre was horrified they would be transmitting to London just down the road from the German top brass, but Antoine, the new *reseau* leader, said it would be safe.

'The Germans will never think to look so close. That's the theory, anyway. We'll just have to keep a watch out for D/F vans. If we see one sniffing about, there's always the wood to run to.'

'It all seems too risky,' Pierre said. 'I'm not happy.'

'OK,' Antoine nodded. 'How about if Bernard transmits sometimes from the far side of the wood, sometimes from a safe house, only rarely from here, perhaps that would be safer? What do you think?'

Perhaps it was a decision which saved their lives. In the fourth week, just two days before they got the 'alert' for D-Day, they heard that a D/F van had been seen close by. At that time Bernard, keeping a 'sked' with London, was transmitting from the village. From time to time the D/F vans cruised round. The *alimentation* in the village was raided in the middle of the night, and an illegal radio was confiscated. Bernard was very good at his job — keeping his transmissions to a minimum, and varying times as much as he could, though it wasn't always easy. In those heady, urgent days leading up to D-Day, it was a temptation to be reckless.

Pierre worried about Rebecca. Was she being careful enough? He had no way of protecting her now.

He heard news of her the night they received the first alert messages over the BBC. In an ideal world, with each *reseau* watertight and independent, he would have heard nothing. But through one of those tiny cracks in the system, so dangerous for security, he did at last have news. An injured W/T operator had been driven across France to them, evacuated from his *reseau* north of Lyons. Theirs was the nearest landing field which was not *brûlé*, useless, burned out, in these dangerous times and they were to get him away.

The operator was in a bad state. There had been no safe doctor nearby, and he had been given only the most basic medical treatment. The group hid him in a stable on one of the outlying farms. Antoine had been a medical orderly with the French Army before being demobbed in 1940. He took off the bandages. New blood began to spurt out of the wound, and the man, semi-conscious and feverish, wouldn't lie still.

'Can you keep an eye on him?' Antoine said to Pierre, pulling his bicycle from its hiding place behind the straw bales. 'I'm going for the doctor in the village. He's a friend and he's helped us before. It'll be OK.'

Pierre stood in the doorway, his sten over his shoulder, watching Antoine cycle up the hill on the far side, beyond the little stream. The thunder of distant bombing had stopped and it was very quiet. There was half-grown green corn in the field in front of the farm. Pierre wondered idly who would harvest it. The injured man seemed to be sleeping, but then he turned to see the man was struggling to sit upright, his eyes bright with fever.

'Would you like water?' Pierre asked. He found the tin cup and the bottle, pouring a little. The man looked at him without speaking.

'The little fox has orders to take over from me.'

'Sorry?'

'They say she was with the *maquis*. She's very brave. She carries a sten, so,' he mimed, awkwardly, with his good arm. 'They say she's killed ten Boches. She has sharp teeth.'

'What do they call her?' Pierre asked, his heart thudding, knowing that it wouldn't mean anything.

'Françoise. They say she came from England. They told her she had to leave the *maquis*. She was their operator for a while. Our *reseau* is very important, you see, and we have to have a good "pianist". I was wounded, so she took over from me.'

He tossed and turned feverishly, muttering to himself. He sat up again.

'She'll be in the middle of the fighting. That's what she wants. She's fierce, that little fox. Very dangerous now. Five of us have been taken in the last year. She doesn't care. She tosses that red hair. We all like her.'

Pierre filled the cup again, wondering fast how he might get to Lyons, take her away, anywhere, up into the hills, take her to the *maquis* where they had been happy, anywhere, disobey orders, anything, anywhere. Out of danger.

When the doctor had done his best for the injured man and left, they drank *marc* in the kitchen on the farm, and listened to the BBC. The stand-by messages came through for them for D-Day, to prepare for action on the fifth June.

He could no longer hope to reach her.

21

The wounded man was picked up by Hudson from the 'Olive' field north of the village. Four days later, final messages came through for action that night, fifth June. Two groups blew up the Paris line and demolished a bridge over the main road. The following morning, taking a late breakfast in Antoine's kitchen, they heard the first news on the radio of the landings in Normandy. Antoine brought out an old bottle of liqueur, with a kick like schnapps, which his wife had distilled in the cowshed. They drank a toast to the Allied victory, expecting to be liberated within days.

A courier cycled in after dark. He was shaking, white-faced.

'It's like Armageddon! Never seen anything like it. You could walk from the sea to the cliffs on soldiers. Most of the poor sods are dead. And the colour of the sea — you wouldn't believe it. So much blood! I used to take my kids down there in the summer; we'd go cockling for our suppers. I'll never take them there again. You couldn't forget that sight, long as you live!'

He collapsed in a chair. 'Those poor buggers! They don't stand a chance. Bastards are just mowing them down. Throwing everything at them. They're being cut to pieces. I tell you, if this is the last push, there's no chance for any of us. There won't be anything left. And they just keep coming! They must have guts, those blokes! And the sea's rough. They're wallowing about like porpoises in those flat boats; then they have to get out and swim for it, with the Boches chucking everything at them. I wouldn't be down there for a million francs, facing that lot. I was up in a crack in the cliff, looking down. I got out of there quick. We don't stand a chance!'

They seemed to be in some kind of limbo, cut off. No more messages came through Bernard. The days dragged on. No one came to arrest them, and no German troops arrived.

Then Bernard began receiving messages from England again. There were parachute landings around Caen, not so far from the group. They were ordered to disrupt communications as much as possible. Somehow the British and Americans were establishing a bridgehead. It seemed a miracle that the Allies had got ashore, let alone inland. There was a great deal of Allied bombing around Paris. Pierre couldn't stop thinking about Rebecca. Where was she now? Was she safe?

The *maquis* was getting bolder everywhere, with the inevitable reprisals. Pierre's group had a constant struggle to keep the Paris line closed in the face of tight German security. It was dangerous work. In the end, when they took the *gardes voies* off the line and put in the troops, the group had to pull back. But by then, in any case, the bombers had done their work and whole stretches of track were pockmarked with craters of twisted metal, the Germans working every night to get the track clear. Reinforcements were needed for the beachhead, and there were the terrible human cargoes to be sent back to the Fatherland.

They saw them one night, when they had been stalking the track, trying to work out how to blow up the line one last time, with what remained of their explosives. A string of cattle trucks came past on the newly repaired line, then stopped by some obstruction. The guards came out to clear it. In the darkness, as the group hid in the bushes, they heard a desperate animal screaming, taken up by the other trucks. Then one last cry, which would haunt him all his life. The most terrible, the most unspeakable, an anguished cry, the cry for comfort, the night cry, the fear of the dark cry. The cry of a separated child.

Pierre knelt and put his hands over his ears to try to cut it out. But there was no escape. A screech of rusty rollers, and the door of one of the trucks was flung open. The torches of the guards shone on a sea of skeletal faces. The stench of human shit and blood, rotting flesh still on the bone, a gust from Hell itself. It wafted across the track towards them where they lay frozen in the bushes. The guards shouted orders and a whip cracked. The trucks screeched as they moved forward on the tracks.

'My God! It's true, what they say! Les Juifs!' Antoine whispered. 'There are children in there. Did you hear that cry? It doesn't matter about us. If we are caught now, it's nothing! We have to do more!'

**

Bernard was on watch, when a boy cycled up the drive and handed him a slip of paper. It was for Pierre. He read it at the table, in the dim lamplight.

'I am close. I must see you soon. I will come. R.'

'What is it? Come on, tell us. More orders?'

'Nothing, Antoine. It is something else. Personal.' He got up from the table, his head swimming.

Bernard winked. 'I interrogated the lad, but he is only the baker's son. He says the message was passed to his father. That's all he knows. Anyway, they're on our side. A love letter, maybe? Tell me, Antoine! Have you ever seen him with a woman from the village? He's a dark one!'

'Let him alone, Bernard. Come on, do you want to finish this game? I was winning, after all.'

'Can we leave it for now?' Pierre said. 'I'll change watch with you, Bernard. It's so hot. I could do with the air.'

He took his gun and went out of the kitchen.

It was a very clear night. He could see in the rising moon right across the valley, where the village huddled round the church on the far side, lightless in the blackout, the street falling like a silver river down the side of the hill. There were stars behind the black conical shape of the church, very bright.

She could be that near, he thought.

111

Owls called to one another in the wood below the château. He wanted her so much — to speak to her, just to be near, to know she was OK. He didn't know how he could have gone on so long without her, functioning, doing his job. He thought he should go and find her now, before all the terrible things that were happening to people in the war should happen to them both. Now! He wanted to run down the steep drive to the château gates, onto the road, up into the village, into the shining street, shouting her name, till she came out from one of the sleeping houses. She was so real to him then, that night, that whole empty night, he could almost touch her.

The next day and the next, she didn't come. He was trapped in the château, keeping watch as Bernard spent hours transmitting and receiving — sometimes in the château itself, sometimes in the grounds, while they watched from the top floor for the D/F vans. It was very risky but as the Allies advanced, the sabotage activity behind the German lines grew fiercer. Supplies and reinforcements had to be prevented from reaching the front. Bernard was the focal point for endless requests and instructions. The old folk had left weeks before and the château had become an unofficial HQ for all sorts of disorganised Résistance factions who had suddenly come out of the woodwork — les napthalinés, the mothball patriots. He couldn't do what he most wanted to do — look for Rebecca. He had to wait.

Three days later, they heard shelling in the distance. Bernard and Pierre rushed to the top floor of the château. Against the skyline, a German convoy was under attack across the valley. One lorry was exploding in a slow sheet of flame, candled figures jumping out, haloed with light. Pierre felt no pity for them, only exhilaration. Then Antoine, cycling pell-mell up the steep slope on his forbidden bicycle, was shouting at them that the generals were going. They raced to the top of the house again and looked down. Large, pale staff cars speeding past, the faces grim. They knew then it was the beginning of the end.

All day the Allied Bombers drummed the sky. The half-rotten window-frames in the château, empty now because the shutters had been burned for fuel, vibrated in sympathy. Once a Mosquito circuited the grounds, swooping low over the terrace, peppering the stone urns with machine-gun fire, thinking perhaps this was the château in the village where the Germans had billeted their staff officers. Bernard, who had been standing on the steps eating a peach from the south wall, was forced to sprint for the French windows, swearing oaths at the Allies as he ran.

There was a strangeness about that whole day. It was very still and hot, the vibration of the planes a sick wave in his head. Antoine was anti-Gaullist, and he and Bernard had a row about politics in the kitchen. Pierre couldn't stop asking himself what was happening to Rebecca.

At *midi* they had more ripe peaches, and some stale bread. Would there be bread tomorrow? There were more explosions along the route where they had seen fighting that morning. Pierre took his shirt off and sat with his bren, hidden from view of the road but where he could still keep watch. They were all arguing about whether they should take their guns and go to the *maquis*. The château was becoming more dangerous. Bernard had a 'sked' with London. They agreed to go together to the wood behind the house, Antoine keeping watch, perhaps ask London for further instructions. It was risky. Antoine had seen a D/F van cruising the main route that morning. There were still Germans in the village, despite the evacuation of the senior officers. The closeness of the Allies seemed to make them even more determined to winkle out the terrorists.

Pierre went back to the top of the house to keep watch from the window. He could see Bernard and Antoine climbing the wall in the orchard with the W/T set between them, the wood beyond.

The waves of bombers had stopped, and there was no more shelling from behind the ridge. He walked from one window to another, scanning the horizon. At one point he saw a tank career up the village street. Children ran behind it in a cloud of dust.

It was heavy and hot in the old house. Pierre dragged a chair from a far corner and placed it by the window, so that he could keep watch on the orchard.

A German soldier was creeping through the grass towards the château. Another one appeared. In the opposite direction from the orchard, a US soldier appeared over the wall, followed by three others, heads decorated with leaves. The château had become the front line.

Then he saw Rebecca. She was walking through the tawny grass of the orchard towards the house, in a loose summer dress, faded blue, a sub-machine gun on her hip.

There was no time. A platoon of Germans was crawling towards the path, Allied soldiers approaching stealthily from the orchard. Rebecca was no more than fifty yards away, shielded only by the dense growth of the stunted apple tree. She would be caught in the crossfire.

He saw something else in that moment, the wind blowing against her swelling body, the way she held herself, how she walked in her proud glory above the grass.

He had to warn her! In a panic, he tried to open the French windows to the balcony, but some fool had lost the key.

He fired at the lock. At least the gunshot would alert her. Again and again. He saw her look up, surprised, begin to run towards the house. No, no. Run the other way!

The old wood splintered but the door stayed shut. He ran backwards through the room and launched himself through the unopened windows with its splintered glass. Other faces were looking up. Helmets running towards him. Soldiers on the lawn. Guns. The balcony, unused for so many years, since the key was lost, collapsed under his weight and he fell through flights of air.

'Pierre!' She was looking up at him.

A scent of wallflowers mingled velvet and sweet blood.

22

Pierre was dreaming he was a child again in Brittany. He was often alone, fishing in the river which ran through his grandmother's land, the banks fringed with tamarisk trees. He hid there, safe among the fronded branches, watching wading birds feeding in the mud. At low tide, the water combed the green hair of the weed, and he would find tiny crabs hiding from the sun. Crouching by the water, he would try to decide that moment when the slack brown tide, *l'eau mort*, begins to flow upstream. It's a game he played by himself, watching for the moment when the sticks he had laid in the river would be taken forward, slowly at first, then faster and faster, past the tamarisk and the willow on the far bank, until they disappeared from sight, upriver towards his grandmother's house.

It was a lonely childhood, cut off from most of his French family, the illegitimate child of an English captain killed in the First World War. His cousin Marie-Thérèse told him they loved each other and would have got married, but then he was killed at Ypres. He wasn't sure whether to believe her. Whatever the truth, it was still a great disgrace, and that was why he didn't live in the big house, but on the farm instead, with his cousin's family. He had to have a tutor every day, not allowed to go to school. Sometimes his mother took him up to the great house at the head of the river, where an old lady in black rapped his knuckles with a walking stick and made him sit in a corner.

Now, there were white coats, hushed voices. He wondered if he was dying. He could remember nothing after falling from the château windows. Only blackness. Drug-induced dreams took the pain away. And he was glad of the dreams.

Now again he was back at *Le Tamaris*, the yard just as it was. Rebecca's tamarisks, a group of ancient trees, cast feathery shadows on the sunbaked earth. Then he remembered he had never been there in the summer, only in his mind. When he woke again, he understood there would be nothing left. The farm, at the centre of the battle for Normandy, close to the landing beaches, would almost certainly have been destroyed in the Battle of the Bocage.

***

For a long time there was nothing more, only dreams of the past which haunted his sleep. He sat in his chair at the rehabilitation centre; an empty shell marooned by the tide. VE Day came and went. The nurses and the staff put on a party on the lawn, and people came from the village. There was red, white and blue bunting, coloured lights around the doors; music and dancing in the evening. Most of the patients could only watch from their wheelchairs. They moved some of the bed patients onto the terrace; white-sheeted forms still visible in the dusk, among the dancers.

Nothing stirred him, not even the victory. It was too unbearable to think of Rebecca, lost in the ruins of Europe. And had there really been a child? He tried to piece it all together. Those last moments in the château. Occasionally, he would whip himself into action, and for a few days he would write feverish letters to the War Office, and to what remained of SOE. The Colonel came to see him and he badgered him for news. He told Pierre gently there was little hope. So many were unaccounted for; Europe was in chaos. Even so they would surely have heard something by now. The camps were slowly being liberated, but they had better face the facts. There was really no chance she could be alive.

He knew he had to get back to Europe, somehow, where he might find the answer for himself, even if that answer were too terrible to bear. Better to know, better than living in limbo. He began to attend the morning physiotherapy sessions, to take his first steps. As his legs grew stronger, he walked in the grounds obsessively, day after day, until it was too dark to see.

Edward came to visit. The first time Pierre was in a wheelchair on the terrace. Edward glanced at him and averted his eyes, stared out at the ornamental lake.

He coughed nervously.

'Forgive me, Pierre. It's none of my business. But I understand you are thinking of selling your part of your Brittany inheritance.'

'Yes. I've written to my mother's solicitors. They can arrange it.'

'Is that wise just now? After all, old chap, it's your birthright. When you're fully operational again you'll be glad of it — keep your interest going, that sort of thing.'

How could he bear to go back to France without Rebecca? He had heard from others who had returned. The camaraderie was ebbing away. In those last days, the *napthalinés* had come out into the open, making a bid for political power. He remembered the reseaux used to say *We are the resisters of the first hour*. Where were they now?

'I want to forget,' he told Edward. 'France was never my country. My mother left, remember. She made a new life in England, where she was happy. I need to cut the ties.'

'You may feel differently when you are fit again. Just hang on for a bit before you sell. You never know what's round the corner, once you're up and about!'

'Yes, maybe you're right.' Pierre hesitated. 'There is something I need to do first, anyway. I'll get back into Europe, find out some answers. I'm sure they'll give me a job. Then I'll come back home to England and sort everything out for good.'

'That's wise. You've had a terrible prang. Enough to knock a chap sideways. You shouldn't close off all your options now.'

Pierre was silent, staring at the lake. Edward stood hesitating by the window, a plump, greying man in a camelhair coat below his knees, twisting the brim of his hat.

'It's up to you', he said at last, awkwardly. 'But I confess I'd be glad to have you here, in England. I'm on my own now. It's pretty dreary these days, with your mother gone. When they've finished patching you up, how about coming to live with me in Surrey? At least for a bit? I can get some help in for you. Though I dare say,' he added hastily, seeing Pierre's face, 'it won't be needed for long.'

'Thank you. I'll think about it.'

Just before Pierre left, he had another visitor. He had been walking in the grounds, more strongly now. Coming back through the front door, he saw a tall American waiting, in the uniform of a US Army sergeant, his huge frame draped easily in one of the straight-backed chairs in the entrance hall. Somehow, he seemed familiar.

'Captain Beaune?'

The visitor lifted himself out of the chair, extending his hand.

'Hey! I'm real glad to see you again! I've been asking about you everywhere, even phoned your War Office. Some stiff old guy told me to get lost. You were real lucky, you know that? Sure gives me the creeps thinking about it. Where'd they get you, anyway?'

'In the arm. And my legs.'

'Yeh, I knew you were in a bad way. Jumping through that glass, that was kinda stupid.'

'You were there?'

'Yeah! I was there! Me and the other guys, we really thought you'd had it. If we hadn't stopped those Germans from filling you up some more, I guess you would have done duty as a stiff.'

'Thank you. I can't remember anything. It's all a blank, I'm afraid.'

'Hey, that's nothing. Don't thank me. All in the call of duty. I'm being posted back to the US three days' time. Took me this long to find you. You Top Secret or something?'

'No.'

'I tell you, it gives me a real kick, seeing you. We lost a lot of men in our platoon. Takes some getting over. It's a good feeling, knowing you got through OK. You make something of it, d'you hear? Just having a smashed-in face, don't stop no one havin' a good time. Say, didn't they do none of that plastic surgery on you?'

Pierre found himself smiling. It hurt.

'Yes. This is the result!'

'Well,' he drawled, studying him with his head on one side. 'Sure thing, they made a mess of you. Guess it was worse before they started patching you up?'

Pierre grinned again, feeling the stiff muscles.

'I suppose it was.'

'Hey, I gotta go! It's been great seeing you. I'll tell the guys!' He looked at Pierre anxiously. 'You be OK now?'

'Yes, I'll be OK. Thanks.'

He got to the door.

Pierre swallowed hard. 'That day. There was a girl, she was coming to meet me. Do you know what happened to her?'

'Sure thing! Hey, that girl was somethin'! The way she held them bastards off, reckon she was the one really saved your life!'

For a moment the world hung in the balance.

'She had some pluck, kneeling over you and giving them hell with her machine gun. What a doll! Must've taken out three or four before they got her!'

'So she was ... shot? They killed her?'

The tick of the clock.

'No way! Took her with them. Grabbed her and held her in front of the lead guy as a hostage, the cowards. We didn't dare fire on them. A pregnant woman — says something about them arseholes, 'scusing my language. Using a woman like that. We went after them soon as we could, but they got away. We were in the middle of another battle straight off. Plumb in the front line for a while.'

Pierre went with him to the door, walking down the steps with some difficulty. The sergeant punched him in his good arm.

'Like I say, you got a second chance! Lucky guy! Real shame about the girl. I wonder what happened to her? Guess we'll never know.'

Pierre shook his hand again, struggling to find the words to thank him, words which wouldn't come. He watched the jeep until it disappeared round the bend in the drive.

23

Tsura was whispering.

'We made a promise — do you remember?'

Five of them, crushed into one thin bunk, the stink of old rags. Only their body heat, in this bitter winter, keeping them alive.

Marie was trying to feed from Rebecca, but her breasts were flat. Soon she would start to cry. 'Shhh. They'll hear!'

'We're sisters, aren't we? We promised to take care of each other's children, if the worst should happen.'

Tsura put her arms around Rebecca's neck, and leant her head against her. Rebecca could hear her whispering through her bones.

'I am Roma. I know things, sometimes far into the future, sometimes tomorrow. You know I have the Sight.'

There was a stirring at the far end of the hut, a groan, the splatter of diarrhoea on the floor. Some poor creature, caught again. If the guards arrived, they would all have to get up.

With her own body, she felt Tsura's thinness.

'Tell me quickly. What is it?'

'The war is almost over — just a few more days. Then the Russians will come. I will be among the last. They'll take me to the gas chambers. We all know what happens. That's where I'll go tomorrow.'

'Shut up! I'm trying to sleep!' The woman next to Rebecca on her other side hissed in the blackness.

'Would you keep Aishe for me? I've hidden her under the hut. I gave her my ration of bread two days ago and I told the guard she'd died. They didn't bother to look.'

That splatter of diarrhoea again, another groan.

'You will survive, Rebecca. You and your child. Somewhere, you will survive. But I will not. There is a future for both our children somewhere. It isn't clear, but I can see it.'

That whisper again on her other side. 'I said, shut up! We don't want the guards in here!'

There were footsteps outside the door. A fat woman outlined against the pale night, snow still falling. The torch shone in.

'Someone has shat in here; some animal. You will all be beaten! Get up. Get up! Get on your filthy hands and knees. Clean the floor with your hands! Then tell me, who is it? We'll take her away for treatment.'

Laughter in the dark. Terrible. Chilling.

'Good treatment! In the recovery room, for shitting a filthy pile on my clean floor. Now tell me, you animals. Tell me who it is. Otherwise, we will beat you all.'

The hut was silent.

At first light, when they had cleaned the floor and wiped their hands on the rags that covered them, Tsura was taken away. Her name in Romany, she had told them, meant 'light of dawn'. She was a singer.

***

'They're running around like headless chickens.' Frieda whispered to Rebecca. 'They're taking the women away. And any children that are left. Something must be happening.'

'They say the Russians are almost at the camp. They'll be panicking. They don't want any evidence left behind. They'll kill us all.'

The whisper ran down the line. The dogs heard it, and snarling, attacked the last woman in the queue. The guards were laughing, entertained. The women shuffled forward to get their cup of imitation coffee before they started work. Rebecca clutched Marie close. The only reason she had survived so far was because they thought she could be the child of a SS officer. A useful lie. That 'invitation' to dinner with the man with the lizard tongue, recorded obsessively in some bureaucratic file.

Requests for procurement of local women. The invitation she never accepted. Still there, though, in the meticulous records of the SS. Rebecca got extra rations occasionally which she would share. To begin with, the other women prisoners avoided her, thinking her a collaborator, but soon they understood that it was only a lie, perpetuated for her survival, and that of the child. The guards treated her like a slut, with that strange twisted thinking which enabled them to do what they did. Rebecca was next for the brothel, if they had time to send her. The child, part Aryan, they believed, so far they had allowed to survive. Who would have thought the SS officer with the lizard tongue would save their lives?

'Where is Aishe?' someone whispered, urgently.

'Still under the wall,' she whispered back, looking at the ground, as she shuffled forward.

'Give her this when you can.' A morsel of bread passed into Rebecca's hand.

Most of them in the line wore the red triangle, for political prisoners, ex-members of the Résistance. There were several French in her group. They were not sure how to categorise Rebecca. Even though she had shot at them, she claimed it was only in self-defence to protect her precious child — the child of an SS officer. If they had known Rebecca was a 'pianist', she would have been tortured and executed by now, hung up by wire. It was so lucky she hadn't had her W/T set with her that day. So she clung on, half-alive. Those who wore the black triangles, the gypsies like Tsura, the lesbians, the social deviants, had all gone. And the Jews, of course. The first to go. Rebecca thought of her Jewish great-grandmother, and thanked her grandfather with all her heart for his clever papers. So far, so far…

***

Four of the women guards herded them into a long line, with blows from their rifle butts and snatched, hungry bites from the dogs. One woman protested, and Gerda, the worst of them, knocked her to the ground. Rebecca and another woman picked her up. She was so light, blood streaming from a head wound. Then the gates were opened onto a landscape thick with snow.

'They are sending us out in that! They must be scared. The cold will kill us anyway!'

'What have we got to lose? If we stay, we'll die. They don't want anybody left alive to tell them what happened. At least we've got a chance. And whatever happens, we must save the children.'

'But maybe they will shoot us in the snow.'

The long, long march north-west towards Mecklenburg. Thousands. Women who at the last call had survived the gas chambers. There were other women in the camp left behind, some of them French. Whoever they were, they had all become sisters. Perhaps they had a chance out in the bitter snow, but those left behind had none, unless the Russians came soon.

***

The guards were not paying attention. They were nervous and jumpy, shooting one woman when she tried to pee in the snow. But now Rebecca noticed they were not watching, and as she came close to a village, she took her chance. The others, understanding what she was going to do, created a diversion, a fight in the snow. All the guards had their backs to Rebecca now, screaming abuse, kicking at the three women fighting. She took her chance. Grabbing Aishe by the hand and, clutching Marie to her chest, she ran with all she had left, weak after the typhus. There was a huge snowdrift just ahead and she pulled Aishe behind it. There were shots, the dogs barking. Were they for her? If so, they had no hope.

They lay in the snowdrift. Marie was crying. Rebecca pushed the child's face against her chest, almost to suffocation. Aishe was quiet, clutching Rebecca's hand. She seemed to understand.

Rebecca looked back to where the long, trampled line had marked the snow. Miraculously the march had passed into the white distance, but there was more blood in the snow, a crumpled body. Someone had given a life for them, so they could have a chance.

In the dusk, in bitter cold, clutching the children to her, Rebecca could see the outline of a church. The little square was deserted, the cobbles rimed with ice, dirty snow holed up in gutters, a feeling of hopelessness. She crawled up the steps, and banged on the closed door.

It opened. A man held his arms out, his black cassock billowing in the wind.

'Come!'

***

But then the Russians came.

'I found this lot, hiding in the crypt!' A soldier with a gun, pointing at them.

'Leave them alone! They are in sanctuary, in God's house!' The priest stood in front of the children. They were huddled together on the floor with Rebecca. He was holding out his black cassock, protecting those under his wings.

'I repeat, this is God's house! Please. You are good men. Do not despoil his house, I beg you!'

The Russians had pushed into the church. The village had been waiting for days, during which the priest had hidden them. Other children were hidden in attics and barns around the village, the whole population waiting in terror. The stories had gone before the liberators; grandmothers hung from trees, women raped, men butchered before their families' eyes. Yet no one expected them to violate the sanctuary of the church. But here they were.

A soldier pushed the priest aside and when he resisted, hit him with the butt of his gun, once, twice. He fell on the altar steps. The children screamed.

The soldier made a lunge for the children, and the priest staggered back to his feet, to head him off. The soldier came at him again, and Rebecca ran in front of him, striking out, biting and kicking. The children were wrapped in each other's arms. Then a curt command. An officer, gold-braided, strode down the aisle. Rebecca was aware of his eyes on her.

Something passed between them, those two men — some arcane agreement. Another command. The soldier saluted.

The officer said something in Russian, then in German.

'She might do for me, when she is cleaned up! Keep your hands off her! I'll take her for myself!'

Somehow Rebecca found the courage. She held up her hand.

'I will come with you freely, if you give me your word as an officer in the Russian Army you will leave the priest alone, and my children will be safe.'

There was a pause. He nodded.

'Wait! I must write something! Then I will go with you.'

The officer hesitated, and then nodded again. The soldier lowered his gun.

There was a prayer book in the front pew, and she tore out pages hastily. The officer was watching. He unbuttoned his tunic, feeling in his breast pocket. An elegant gold pen. So incongruous in that dim church, with the children crying.

She wrote quickly, a few sentences. Underlined heavily.

'Hurry up!' The officer was tapping his foot.

'I am finished now.'

She handed the paper to the priest. He was slumped on the step, stopping blood with the edge of his cassock

'Keep this letter! And please look after my children. You must take them to a safe place. Then you must find Pierre Beaune, if you can. I have written it there. You must ask the British Army. You must ask the Occupying Forces. They will find him if he is still alive. Give him this note. He will understand. Then he will come to find his children. I have written here that he is the father of Marie, and that Aishe is my adopted daughter. It may help a little in the future. I have written here, too, that you are their guardian, until then. A sacred trust. Please.'

She reached out her arms for the children, but one of the soldiers pushed her back.

The officer shouted.

'That's enough! Leave her alone!'

She held them to her one last time, feeling their fragile warmth, the little bones.

'Be good children! Take care of each other!'

'Go!'

24

The Colonel met Pierre on the stairs. Clerks were running about with files. Everywhere there were workmen unscrewing fixtures, dismantling filing cabinets. There was no office free so they sat in the small kitchen, looking out of a grimy window. The Colonel told Pierre what he had found. After her capture in Normandy, Rebecca had been sent to a camp in the Eastern Sector in the last days of the war. They thought it was possibly Ravensbrück, the women's camp. Since then, nothing.

'Thank God, we don't think the Germans knew she was one of our agents, not unless someone spilled the beans. Luckily, she didn't have her W/T set with her, so hopefully they thought she was part of a splinter group. There were a lot of them about in those last days. That's bad enough. The women agents have had a particularly bad time after capture. If they did identify her as one of our wireless operators, it would have been rather difficult for her. But I'm sorry. We would have heard something by now. I'm afraid it's pretty hopeless.'

He came across and put his hand on Pierre's shoulder, awkwardly. Then he opened the door and shouted for one of the corporals.

'I think you had better have this now. Rebecca put you down as her next of kin. Did you know?'

'No. I didn't know.'

The corporal brought in one of those fibre suitcases the agents lodged with SOE, in case the agents didn't come back. Then they left him alone.

Pierre sat for a few moments, looking out into the courtyard, watching papers burn on a bonfire. Then he opened the case. A tweed suit with a good London label, carefully folded, several pairs of silk stockings, some shoes, a set of lacy underwear. She must have bought them with her first pay, excited to have lovely things, hard to get hold of in England, but harder still in Occupied France. Because of their English labels, she would have had to leave them behind. Between the clothes, sachets of some sweet-smelling herb — lavender he thought, or rosemary. Underneath, a long, legal envelope, then another, smaller, addressed to him — Pierre Beaune. At the beginning of their time in Suffolk, he had told her all about himself. This was dangerous, of course. Unwise. But for the first time between them, nothing was hidden.

He broke the seal on the smaller envelope. A little package, wrapped in silk, fell to the floor. He bent to pick it up and unwrapped it. It was a ring. A blue stone, a sapphire perhaps, surrounded by diamonds. He had never seen it before. Had she brought it with her from France? Carried it with her all the time, secretly?

My darling Pierre, I am to be sent to another part of France, and we won't be together after all. If I don't come back, if we don't see each other again, I am leaving Le Tamaris to you. It's important that a little piece of this earth belongs to us, don't you think? It is what we are fighting for. I have managed to 'wangle' (here she used the English word — she must have picked it up somewhere) a trip by felucca, rather than a parachute jump, as I think I may be pregnant with our child. If that is so, I pray he or she will be born safely in France. Perhaps by then the war will be over. We must hope for that. I will send word, so that you can find me. Be sure that I will take great care, but we will go on fighting, until there is no more need to fight.

However, if you are reading this letter, it must mean that these unimaginable things have come about. If that is so, rebuild the peace at Le Tamaris, for us both. You will have found the ring inside the letter. I don't like to take it back with me. It is for you to keep, as a memory of me. And of Papi, who gave it to me on my birthday. It was my grandmother's ring. I pray that one day we will be reunited, in some other life. That something will return to us one day ... by some miracle.

On the will, the wax seal was already broken. In accordance with procedure, it had been checked by the office, in case anyone had to be contacted. It would have been written just before she went back to France, for the last time, with F Section. She had left him everything. The farm. The old horse, if it survived. The little trawler she used to fish from. She must have thought of all that before she left, carefully. So there would be something left, if she didn't return.

He had always imagined she had gone north in the staff car to catch that last plane, for that last jump into the night. But she had never stayed in the country house, where he had imagined her, sitting in corners, walking in the gardens. Instead, somehow, she had 'wangled' the night trip in the felucca, a submarine landing her in France, because she might be pregnant with their child, and she didn't want to jump.

It seemed a long time. His tea had gone cold. A storm came up. Short bursts of hail hurled themselves against the grimy window. The man who was feeding the bonfire in the yard had left. Half-burnt, shredded paper lifted on the wind and floated past the window. The corporal put his head round the door.

'Are you alright, sir?'

'Yes. Fine. Thank you.'

'The Colonel has got his office back now, sir. Would you like to come along?'

The Colonel was standing halfway on to the window, lifting the gauzy curtain, watching the lunchtime traffic rumbling below.

'Can you get me over there?'

'Into the Eastern Zone? No chance, I'm afraid.'

'I've got to do something. There may be a child.'

'I've contacted our organisations over there already and the Swedish Red Cross. They've much more chance of finding someone. There were so many prisoners, so many orphans. But most children didn't make it, I'm afraid. If they were born in the camps, the Germans were pretty brutal. Occasionally a child survived. Two so far have made it to the Red Cross. But in any case, after what she went through, I doubt there would have been a child. And what chance would it have had?'

'But do you think Rebecca ... or the child ... by some miracle, could be in one of the Red Cross camps?' He was grasping at straws, desperate for hope.

He shook his head.

'I'm sorry! It would be better to face it. We would have heard something by now, though it's absolute turmoil over there. Will be for a while. We'll get it sorted out in the end, but God knows when. If Ravensbrück weren't in the Eastern Sector, it wouldn't be so tricky, but there it is. Relations aren't too good at the moment. The Russians liberated some of the camps, but they aren't giving up all the internees. Some women from Ravensbrück had been sent on a 'death march' by their guards when the Russians arrived. Those barbarians — sending sick and starving women out into the snow! Most of them died, of course. A few got through to the Swedish Red Cross, but Rebecca was not among them. No record at all. Believe me, we've checked. The Germans did their best to cover their tracks; burned a lot of papers. So the records are incomplete and it's impossible to know what's really gone on.'

Pierre moved across to join him at the window. He too stared down at the slow, hiccoughing traffic below.

After a pause, the Colonel walked over to the drinks cabinet.

'Thank God they've left this behind. Better than bloody tea. What'll you have?'

'Whisky, please.'

'I'm afraid we haven't any ice.'

'I need to do something. After all, I'm pretty fit now.'

'I don't suppose the doctors would agree with you.'

'I may be on sick leave, but I still hold a commission. You must have something for me.'

He sighed.

'I'll see what I can do. They're desperate for people to work with the POWs out there; process all the paperwork, that kind of thing. And, I suppose if you have German and French, you could be useful. Go home and wait. I'll do what I can. Just be patient.'

They shook hands and said goodbye. Pierre walked out into the spring sunshine, carrying Rebecca's case. Girls in bright blouses were shopping in their lunch hour. Lovers were walking through the park opposite, arm in arm. He crossed the road in front of a London bus. Where the wind blew in the gaps between burned buildings, he could smell the soot. But there were crocuses in the grass. Cherry blossom lay like confetti along the pavement, and new leaves were appearing on the blackened plane trees. He would go to Germany, anywhere, get hold of documents, buy a car, go and look for himself. Never give up hope. Maybe he would go back to *Le Tamaris*. The farm she had left him. There wouldn't be much left after the fighting in the *bocage*. But there would be the land. The land, and the farm she had loved. If in the end there was no hope, maybe there would still be something left of her, after all.

***

The Colonel asked to see Pierre again.

'Glad you're feeling better, old chap. Legs improving? Good. Now you've been cleared by the MO, I've managed to get you a posting to Cologne. As a Liaison Officer working in the British and French Zones, helping with the repatriation. That kind of thing. Best to get back into it, eh? Stops you thinking too much. Great help.'

'Thank you, sir. I appreciate it.'

Pierre turned to leave.

'By the way, one of our French agents, in his debrief, said he saw Rebecca. He recognised her. She'd been the 'pianist' in his *reseau*. Saw her through the wire, when he was on a work detail. I'm afraid she looked in pretty bad shape.'

'Which camp? Did she have a child with her?'

'He didn't say anything about a child. But it was definitely Ravensbrück. He was in a sub-camp for men attached to the women's camp. Then he was moved on.'

He handed Pierre a file.

'Take that away and have a look at it. It's the info on that job. You'll have to go through yet another medical, I'm afraid. Just a formality. They'll be glad to take on anyone who can speak a couple of languages and isn't completely gaga.'

They shook hands.

'We worry about you chaps, you know. I suppose you saw in the papers about...?'

'Yes.'

'Bad business. Can understand it though. Nothing to hope for. Don't let things get you down. Always here. Well, if not here, in some corner somewhere. Get in touch.'

Pierre went out into the evening rush hour. People were queuing for the theatre. A summer evening in London. Life coming back, like blood into a limb. Except that he was still dying.

25

The driver manouevred the jeep through the empty streets. Every few yards he had to use the wipers to clear the screen. There was grey dust everywhere, the legacy of the bombing.

'Is it all like this?' Pierre shouted over the roar of the engine.

'Pretty much, sir!' the corporal shouted back. 'It's a fucking nightmare!'

Pierre peered through the dusty window. A stark stage set. The fronts of houses with nothing behind but rubble. Empty doorways. A shuffling, grey city of ghosts.

A small girl sat in the road. The driver hooted but she didn't move. She came up to the window.

'Give me gum, chum! Give me cigarettes!'

'Poor kid!' The driver said. 'She's the same age as my daughter back home. They'll beg for anything, sir! Steal if they can. You have to watch them.'

Diggers were moving rubble off the road where a house had collapsed. A woman was lying spreadeagled in the dirt on the side of the road, screaming.

'I think she's in trouble. Can we stop?'

'Don't stop, sir. It's not a good idea. This isn't a good district.'

A Red Cross worker was clambering over the rubble towards the woman.

There was a traffic jam at the junction ahead. No one was going anywhere. People were shouting. Cars and military vehicles trying to get through, making it worse.

'Is it always so bad?'

'Worse usually, sir.'

The Red Cross worker was bending over the woman.

'We have got transport. We could get her to hospital.'

'OK sir.' He sounded resigned. 'I'm supposed to get you to your office by 3 pm for your first briefing. With the major, sir!'

'Just hang on there!'

Pierre jumped out of the jeep and clambered over the broken stone. The dust rose up in clouds. Everywhere horns were blaring, the crash of masonry falling into the waiting lorries. What a place!

'Can we help? We have transport!' he said in faltering German.

The Red Cross worker looked up.

'Thank you! I was just passing! I've only got my bike. She's having it now, I think. Poor woman. She hasn't anywhere to go.'

A small crowd had gathered. The woman screamed again.

'If you could hold her hand, sir! It might help.'

Pierre looked up. Two rats, sharp inquisitive eyes looking down on them from a pile of stones.

'There are rats!'

'Yes. Always. We need to be quick!'

Suddenly there was blood, a slippery creature born into the hands of the waiting worker.

'It's a boy, madam!'

The woman smiled weakly.

'I've radioed for a stretcher but there's gridlock everywhere. Maybe you could get through in the Army jeep, sir? I can follow on my bike.'

They half-carried the woman to the waiting jeep. Pierre took off his uniform jacket and wrapped it round her.

'OK, corporal. Let's see if we can get through!'

It was a bumpy ride through alleyways and over broken masonry, where houses teetered over them, threatening to fall. Children looked out from doorways or from upstairs windows. Women beckoned to them. Old men shuffled through the dust.

At last, they screeched to a halt outside the hospital. They lifted the woman out, the baby in her arms. She was quite young, though her hair was white with dust. She held the baby tightly to her, wrapped in Pierre's jacket.

'Thank you!' she said.

The Red Cross worker arrived on his bike, panting after the ride.

'They'll take care of you now!' He took the woman's arm.

'You did well there, corporal,' Pierre said, clambering back into the jeep.

'Yes, sir. But you're late for your briefing, sir.'

A poky office in a portacabin. Pierre's uniform jacket covered in blood. The Major was unsympathetic. It wasn't a good beginning.

DPs. Displaced Persons. A slack-eyed army of the lost, an endless queue begging for papers, food, clothing, identity, comfort, above all, nationality.

He was besieged. But when he could, Pierre enquired about Rebecca. They gave him the answers they thought he wanted to hear.

'Thank you, sir. I saw that lady in Dresden and Belsen, in Dachau and at Stettiner Railway Station. Yes, she had red hair. She carried a little child.'

There were so many lost women, so many lost children.

26

A letter arrived on his desk, forwarded from Baker Street. A note from someone in SOE.

Sorry this has taken so long to get to you. Chaps in the field sent it back to us. Last year, someone handed it to one of our men on a Judex mission. Russian prisoners, some Polish soldiers, Italians, mixed bag. Apparently, a truckload of these Poles was just off to the Ukraine. Judex chap was visiting a camp for aliens. We've had it translated.

On the envelope some words in an unfamiliar script; the envelope torn, resealed with an official seal. He broke it, pulling out a wad of paper, torn sheets, some blue sugar paper, all covered in the same script, close-written on the page. A typed translation:

Dear Captain, You know me as Boris, from the camp at Neufontelle commanded by Lieutenant Philippe. My true name is Janusz Roucek. I am a Pole from the Ukraine. If this letter reaches you in time, I implore you to help us. We wish to stay in France and make our home here among the people. Perhaps we are to be sent to Russia. Where our homes were, there is nothing. Only Russia. Fifteen of us here have lost all our families, even our country. As an officer of the Intelligence Service, please help us.

I was a student in Warsaw during the first year of the war. Groups of us formed the Résistance, but we were captured by the Germans. I was sent, in an exchange of prisoners, across the frontier with Russia. Later we were sent back again as cannon fodder against the Germans. If you ask a man now if he has been on the Russian front, he will answer you by standing on the toe of his own boot. You will see by the dent what the cold did to us, as you have seen it written on my face. I was taken again by the enemy and sent to France to build the Wall. The Russian prisoners were treated worse than any.

I am writing this every night in my bunk in the camp. Perhaps you will never read these words. Perhaps you too are dead — the only

*powerful Englishman I know. Perhaps you too have been left on a tree
to die. But I must write all that is in my heart, because I cannot tell
anyone. My fellow prisoners find paper for me to write. The Allies
are good to us. They give us food. But they cannot give us a country
where we belong.*

*Three times I have been a prisoner of the Germans. There is a
coldness about them. It is a thing to inspire fear. But the Russians
too, I have found, have terrible cruelty. The barbarity of anger.*

*I have stopped now for three days because I have no more paper.
But a parcel of sugar has come from the Red Cross, and more paper.
Even a pencil. So I am beginning again.*

*After you had left the camp at Neufontelle, there was a drop of
boots, arms and food. You were spoken of as a saint! We made two
raids on the town, but stupid Petit Henri killed a German. Three days
later troops came to our camp in the night. I am glad you were not
there, Captain. They strung up every maquisard from the trees around
in the forest, then when they were half-dead, they set fire to them. I
cannot tell you more about it. They did not kill me because Philippe
insisted I was a German they had taken prisoner. He was very clever.
They were not sure, because I couldn't talk. But I wanted to die with
my friends.*

*They also kept the pretty boy, Marc, who should have been a girl.
Do you remember him? He used to sing in the camp. I think they
wanted him for their own games. It would be better to hang from a
tree. While they were doing things to the bodies, I ran into the trees. I
took Marc with me and we hid for some days in the forest. But I must
tell you a terrible thing. The boy died. He had such terror after what
he had seen he couldn't bear to live.*

*At last, they caught me, and took me in a cattle truck to Germany.
They were in a great hurry because the Allies had landed in the west.
I was sent to East Prussia for labour, and put in a camp there. There
were many women working, making munitions for the front. After
two months I saw a girl. She had a baby. It was Rebecca. I knew her
though she was very thin and her head was shaved. She had been*

moved from Auschwitz, they said, with other French prisoners. They worked her very hard. The other women had told the Commandant the child's father was a German officer in the SS. It was a story she had invented to protect the child. We saved rations for her when we could. At that time the child was alive. It was a girl.

Pierre stood up from his desk, and went out into the corridor, leaning against the wall. Clerks hurried past him with files. Then he went back into his office. He had dropped the papers on the floor. He gathered them up and began to read again.

I managed to contact Rebecca in October after the child was born. It was a time of great danger. The Germans were running amok. The Russians were rumoured to have broken through into East Prussia, committing terrible atrocities. No one was spared. The population was fleeing. Things became bad. Perhaps we would be shot by the guards. We were starving. I sent a message to Rebecca in the women's camp at Ravensbrück. The message came from another of the women in her 'family' that she was ill with typhus.

In the end our guards deserted us. We broke out into the Prussian winter. All Germany was fleeing in terror from the Reds. Terrible stories of rape, children being murdered before the eyes of their parents. Allied prisoners, they said, were being butchered with the rest. Some women had got away with the Red Cross. Some had been sent out into the snow to die. I heard more news of her. She had another child with her, one she was taking care of, though she was very ill. I got a message to her at last, to tell her I would protect her. But she sent a message back begging me to get back to France somehow, to find you, to tell you about the children. She thought she would die soon.

Finally, I had to leave with the others. It was hard for me. I can tell you now, I loved her too. We had a hard journey. The Germans who travelled beside us — the old women, the very young, became our friends; everywhere the German peasants shared bread with us. Can they have known what had been done in their name? I think many of them did know. I cannot forgive them for that. It was a difficult journey — always the machine guns of the Russian planes, snow and

melting ice on the rivers, only this time it was not cold enough to
cross. At last, we found the safety of the American lines. It was safety
for some but not for me.

We are to be taken away soon. Perhaps, it will be too late for your
help to reach me. It is only important that you should know about
Rebecca. I know you will understand that I loved her. Please try to
find her and the child.

My respects to you, my captain

Janusz Roucek.

Pierre put in a priority call to HQ in London, and got through
at last to the boffin who had translated the letter.

'What happened to the man? Do you have any idea?'

'No idea. Sorry. The letter was from an internment camp,
with an internal note from an official. *Don't know what to do
about this. Any suggestions?* Usual thing, but what can you do?
Apparently, the queue was lining up at the showers. Suddenly
there's this commotion. A man with some appalling disease,
half his face eaten away, breaks ranks and comes running up to
our chap, thrusts an envelope under his nose. All he can do is
grunt, and all his fellows were laughing.

'Chap didn't know what to make of it. Anyway, he took
the envelope to the Camp Commander but he couldn't read
Polish either, so finally it was sent here under the heading of
Intelligence. Means no one in the field has a clue. That's usually
when we get landed with the hot potatoes. I translated it and
took the decision to send a message to our man from the Judex
mission. He went back into the camp to try and find the poor
chap, but Mr Roucek had been deported. Unknown destination,
I'm afraid. He must have been sent behind the Russian lines. We
tried our best, but you know the political situation. Everyone's
treading on eggshells.'

Pierre made more enquiries, but it seemed Boris was behind
that Iron Curtain Churchill had spoken about in his speech in
Berlin. Untraceable. Lost.

27

Sitting at his desk in Cologne, in the sick heat of the ruined city, Pierre was drinking sour coffee when a corporal brought a priest into the room. Pierre had been seeing DPs all morning. Most he couldn't help. He had seen priests before. They usually came to beg for something for themselves or, rarely, for someone else. Pierre left him standing while he read an unnecessary memo, catching the nasty habits of bureaucracy. Then he looked up. A tall, middle-aged man with a grey face, a German jowl which once had been fat, a thin cassock hanging in folds. A big man, strongly made, but some curious collapse had folded him inwards. He said something in German, then in English with a thick German accent. Pierre waved at him, dismissively.

'This is the French section. We deal with French nationals here.'

The priest stood there, looking at Pierre. His mind played back the priest's words.

'I'm sorry! They told me I would find you here. I heard you were asking about Rebecca.'

Pierre sank back into his chair. 'I'm sorry. It's been a bad day. You must know, I've been asking … everywhere.'

The priest bent down from his great height, watching Pierre's face.

'We were looking for you too. Because of this.' He held out some paper, thin, like the pages from a hymn book, or a prayer book. 'Take it! Read it!'

Pierre leaned over and took the paper.

He was the father of a child. A girl. She had named the child Marie.

'I am Father Ruch. For Rebecca, you must not have any hope. It is important to understand. But the child is still alive. Rebecca made me promise to take care of her. And another child. Aishe. Rebecca adopted her. Her mother was a Roma woman. She went to the gas chambers.'

***

Pierre didn't want to let the priest out of his sight. Father Ruch had come in from the country two days before. Pierre tried to find him a bed in the Mess, so he wouldn't leave, but he refused. Pierre was frightened he might never see him again.

He said yes to everything. Did he have a car? Petrol? They would go to the orphanage where the child was being cared for. He would ask for compassionate leave. There were no telephones working in the countryside. Father Ruch must send a message somehow. There would be papers to sign. In this city of bureaucracy, there would still be papers. It would all take time.

'I will come again. Don't worry! I just wanted to be sure. I won't go away. I am needed elsewhere at the moment. But I will come soon. Trust me.'

Five more people to see that day. Between interviews, he took the thin scraps of paper and read them endlessly. They were thin as tissue, torn from a hymn book. Her writing there, just a scrawl across pages.

He went back to his billet, had a bath in a few inches of water. A child, still alive. A girl. A child like Rebecca. Marie. He said the name for the first time to himself, giving her life.

He lay in the dark. Perhaps she would have Rebecca's hair — red-gold. She had cut off her hair. She was always too thin. Too thin to have a child.

He didn't know anything about children. He didn't know how to look after a child.

That night he slept with the paper under his pillow.

28

Two weeks later Father Ruch was standing in the foyer when Pierre came down for breakfast. He removed his battered hat, and stood, that same collapsed look, the same dusty cassock with the frayed hem.

'I came back, as I promised.'

'Have you had breakfast?'

'Breakfast...?' He said the word over. 'Ah, breakfast. Well, perhaps some coffee...'

They sat in the Mess dining room, Father Ruch clutching his hat to him like a badge.

'Is it alright for me to be here? I feel uncomfortable. After all, I am still the enemy.'

Pierre looked at him, startled.

'I'll just say you're on official business if anyone asks. It isn't so strict nowadays.' But the reminder had made an awkwardness between them. The priest had a deep, resonant voice and no doubt could be heard right across the dining room.

The steward was standing at Pierre's elbow.

'Father, will you have some eggs? Still powdered, I'm afraid.'

'No. Thank you. I have eaten already. Last night. With the family of the child.'

'My child?' Pierre went through worlds of feeling in that moment.

'No, no, no. A child who died. She was in a camp for expellees here, in the city.'

He paused. 'I must explain. I am looking after refugees from my district. There are some German families, some survivors from the camps, who must make way now for the new Polish settlers. So we have come here to find a new country. They are being invented all the time. Nuns from my convent have made an orphanage for the war children. We will go there now. Marie is there, and the little Roma child. Her name is Aishe. It means 'alive' in the Romany language. Her mother was killed in the camp — a Romany girl from the south of Germany. All her family had been sent to the gas chambers. It seems Aishe has no one left. Only Marie. Marie is her family now. Rebecca adopted her, and now they are sisters.'

The waiter came, splashing coffee carelessly into the cups. The priest leant over and sniffed the steam. Something Pierre had seen there melted from his face.

'I am very glad to have found you. It has been a great responsibility. Your War Office told us where you were, eventually.' He breathed in and closed his eyes. 'This coffee is wonderful.'

'Is there any chance ... that Rebecca might be alive? Is it true she was in Ravensbrück? What happened to her? I have to know.'

The priest ruffled his grey hair, impatiently. Then, remembering where he was, smoothed it down hastily. Pierre met his direct blue gaze.

'Honestly, I don't know if she could still be alive. But I fear it is almost impossible. She suffered greatly.'

'What do you mean?'

'She escaped from the death march. From the camp. She came to my church. I gave her sanctuary. There was something about her. Some courage, even recklessness. It drew one to her. She didn't care about herself. But the children ... that was different. She would do anything for the children.'

'Did the SS know she had worked for the British?'

'She told me they had begun — you know how they find out such things. I don't have to tell you.'

Pierre's cup crashed down into the saucer. Someone at the next table turned his head.

'She had typhus, of course. In the camp. It left her very weak.'

The priest got up from the table abruptly, catching the white linen cloth under his cassock, spilling the cups. A brown stain of coffee on its whiteness. The dining room was watching.

'Forgive me! Children are starving here, in this city. And I am sitting here, drinking coffee!'

He strode away between the tables. The waiter was coming towards him, plates of bacon and eggs balanced on his arm. There was almost a collision. Pierre followed and caught at his sleeve. He turned, his great bulk blocking the doorway.

'Excuse me,' Father Ruch said. 'I have been impolite. I am uncomfortable here. I will come for you in four days, in the morning. You need to have a car and as much petrol as we can carry. Then we will go to the convent. It's a long journey. Three days, maybe more in these times. The roads are very bad.'

He was halfway through the swing doors when he turned and came back, causing another jam of people on their way to breakfast. He gripped Pierre's arm.

'We will do our best with what we have left. We will travel together.'

29

They drove through the ruined city in a rented car. The priest sat in the front seat, his great knees jammed against the dashboard, holding his hat.

Once, at a checkpoint in the heart of Cologne they were waved down and their papers inspected. They didn't like Father Ruch's papers at all, with their rash of stamps and overstamps, their tattered edges. They wanted to take him into the command post for checking. Pierre said he would vouch for him. At last, they let them through.

'How did you get through all this red tape before?'

'I am a priest,' he said. 'Sooner or later, they will always let me through.'

It took some time to get out of the city. Often, they were held up by American convoys crossing the road. Somehow the outskirts were worse. At least, in the centre, there was rebuilding; the bustle of troops with a sense of mission, teams of POWs picking at the rubble, the roar of bulldozers, construction going on. But, in the suburbs, it was as if the war had just finished that day, the surviving population still wandering down the ruined streets looking for their homes, looking for their dead; children queueing for food handouts from the Swiss; *trummerfrauen*, the women of the ruins, endlessly piling up bricks. There were shacks along the edges of the streets, built with the broken timber from other people's houses; here and there an untouched corner of a square, where old men slept under the dry fountains, and sometimes a truncated church rose from the rubble.

On the way, he told Pierre more.

'As I told you, she was on the death march at the end. When they knew it was finally over, the SS tried to move the women and children out of the camp. So the Allies wouldn't find them, you see. So there would be no evidence. Some of the prisoners from the camp were lucky — they went in the "white buses" with the Swedish Red Cross. Himmler agreed to it. It was all a cover-up — anything to wipe out what they had done.'

Pierre negotiated carefully past a ruined building in the centre of the road; red, arrowed signs round a bomb crater.

'And the other women?'

Father Ruch sighed. 'Many of them, those who were still alive, were sent on that death march towards Mecklenburg. Rebecca carried Marie through the snow, though she was still very weak with typhus. They guarded the women with dogs; the female guards had whips. Rebecca was also caring for the other child, Aishe, whose mother had been killed. All her family were wiped out. As you know, the Führer had a particular hatred of the Roma people, among others — the Jews, especially, but black people, homosexuals, so many groups. Aishe's mother was sent to Auschwitz, to the gas chambers. So Rebecca looked after her daughter; they were in the same "family" in Ravensbrück. They all helped each other. It kept them alive. Really, they were closer than family. The women were wonderful, amongst all that bestiality, that evil. They looked after the children. So each child had a mother. A pact between them all.'

There was a bridge ahead, its broken masonry still lying in the road. Pierre drove gingerly over it. They were both silent, wondering if they would get across the river safely. It was running fast under the bridge.

When they reached the other side, the priest put his hat firmly back on his head, spreading his hands in a gesture of supplication.

'Yes! The women had such compassion. They suffered so much. For myself I cannot even ask God for forgiveness for what we have done. I don't know how to speak to Him any more. In fact, it's true I don't think He is there. Maybe He was only ever there in our imaginations. What we have begun is terrible. I feel the evil will go on forever. I am ashamed to be German.'

'And Rebecca...? What happened?'

'Somehow, she escaped from the march, in the snow. She was helped by the other women. They covered for her, and she got away with both children. It was a miracle. She fled to the village and to my church. I tried to help her and the two children, gave her food for a few days. But then the Russians came, before I could get them away to safety. The officer in charge was a civilised man. He didn't kill the children,' he paused, 'but he took Rebecca. He wouldn't let his men have her, but he took her with him. She was still beautiful, even after the typhus and ... everything. There was very little mercy in those days, you see. The Russians, when they returned, saw what we had done to them. A man who has seen his own mother hanging from a tree will not have much compassion for another's.'

'Did he want her for himself?'

The priest took off his hat again and ran his finger around the brim.

'I don't know. Perhaps not. Perhaps he was a good man. Some of the soldiers would have violated her, I'm sure. They had already taken my housekeeper. She was shopping in the square. She was a good woman. They ripped her skirts from her. But that officer stopped them from doing worse things in my church.'

'But he took Rebecca away?'

'They took her in a truck with them. When she saw they would take her anyway, she asked me to take care of the children, to find you if possible. She wrote it down on the papers I gave you, while one of them was standing there with his gun. You see, for her, both children were hers. She had taken on that responsibility. It didn't make any difference. A promise. And she passed it on to me; a sacred duty. I vowed to take care of them. I have done the best I could.'

They were leaving the last ruins of the city. Here there were undamaged churches in green meadows. As though there had never been a war. But round a bend in the road, there was a camp with its hood-shaped huts and tall watch towers. Crazy twirls of barbed wire and a stench which carried through into the car, through the open windows.

'What sort of camp was that?'

He shakes his head. 'Something terrible. It's full of refugees now. Some of our people are there.'

We pass some long mounds of earth on the right. Some had grass growing on them, but others looked new, and had crosses planted in the dark earth. He looked away. There was silence in the car.

'It's true I have lost my faith,' Father Ruch said at last. 'We are all responsible for bringing this evil into the world. Now I think that God could not have allowed it, if He had been watching. Perhaps He has just turned away. In my heart I feel He doesn't exist. But perhaps He too has died of grief.'

'Did you ever find out anything about Rebecca? Where they had taken her?'

He shrugged his shoulders.

'It was very difficult. After the first wave of Russians had passed, the worst of it, the high commanders came. I think they didn't want to see what the troops were doing, so they came later. I went to the Major who was clearing the camps. I asked to see Rebecca. I asked where they had taken her. They had no reason to take her, except as a prize. They wouldn't tell me anything. A soldier spat on me and called me a Nazi.'

They were travelling through rolling countryside, now touched by autumn colour. In some places, stray bombs, dropped by the Allies and meant for the industry of the Ruhr and Cologne, had dropped on little communities, even churches. There were unexpected craters in the road; ruined farms blown apart, open to the sky. Pierre wondered if the inhabitants had seen the camps as they cycled past on their way to market, whether they had passed the lines of grey figures with their bundles, whether they deserved punishment for turning away, their deliberate unseeing.

They stopped at an untouched village, and drove up into the little square with its cobbled streets. Old men were sitting at tables, smoking and arguing; a normal scene, the sort of thing you would have come across a hundred times before the war. Everyone stopped talking as they got out of the car. The landlord, seeing Pierre's uniform, spoke to him in English, saying he had sausage and beer. He brought out an extra table. The old men watched them eat. The sausage was tough, the beer flat and sour. But they were glad of it. As they drove away the landlord saluted, smiling.

30

Late afternoon. As he drove up a steep hill through the forest, Pierre glimpsed a schloss among the trees.

'We'll have to stop here,' said the priest. 'You can't go any further in the car. We can walk. It isn't very far.'

Pierre locked the car carefully and opening the bonnet, took out the distributor cap. The priest watched him with a smile.

'No one here will take the car. It's not like Köln. This is the country.'

The path was not steep at first, but then it plunged deep into a ravine, choked with bushes and small trees. The priest was panting in front, like the fat man he once was.

'The sisters hid many refugees during the war, before they had to move. Now they have found a new place, and they are sheltering our own order, and a few of the children, for as long as they can. As soon as I could, I brought the children to them for safety. I hope I did the right thing.'

'Marie? And the other little girl? Aishe?' Pierre said the names hesitantly.

Father Ruch stopped on the path, struggling for breath.

'There are so many children. And only a very few Sisters of Mercy. They are getting old. It's hard for them to take care of so many. You must understand. It is not always very good there. It will be better when they have a proper home.'

They crossed the river over a makeshift bridge, where it narrowed into the gorge and was deep and swift. Blocks of stone lay in the river, arches of an older bridge. The priest stopped again to catch his breath.

'You must prepare yourself. The children have had terrible experiences. Many terrible experiences. It will not be what you expect. And maybe you will want to turn away. It is such a responsibility, taking care of a child. I have thought to take them back with me, but I have no home now where I could keep them safe.'

They scrambled up the far bank, where it had crumbled, taking the path with it. The schloss came into view. Broken pillars guarded a pair of rusted iron gates. Ancient eagles looked down on them. There was tall grass where once there had been lawns, a wide expanse of gravel. A brooding place.

'The nuns will be at their afternoon prayers,' he said. 'We won't disturb them.' He led him around the side of the main building, through a kitchen garden. They passed the chapel, set by itself, hard against the wall. Pierre heard a hush of voices rising and falling.

There was a small formal garden beyond, much overgrown. A peacock screamed from the wall. The priest lifted his head, startled, and the bird shook his tail at them.

'I think that bird is the only one that wasn't eaten.'

'Was this a rich place before the war?'

'They took the family away. Some aristocratic family who didn't agree with the Führer. They were arrested and taken to the camps. Then the Sisters came, after it was abandoned. They have been trying to make it into an orphanage. They are good women, but there are only a few of the order left. The Mother Superior was taken and shot after they found a Jewish boy here. They don't always manage so well with the children now. There is not enough discipline among the Sisters. And the helpers are not very experienced. I sometimes think they don't love the children. However, sometimes love is not enough. Soon the authorities will come and take the rest of the children to a new place. I think it will be for the best, in the end, if it can't be made better.'

There was a doorway in the wall. A stone staircase wound upwards to a closed door on a first floor of this little tower, away from the others. There was screaming from behind the door. Father Ruch knocked. The door was opened by an old woman. Pierre saw three children in cots in the dim room. One tiny child screaming, standing in a filthy cot. She was appallingly thin. She had on a huge cloth nappy, but shit was running down her leg and onto the stained mattress. There was a sour smell of diarrhoea. Sharp shoulders, bony legs sprouted from a faded dress which was too short. She stared at them and screamed again. Her head had been shaved, and fine red-brown hair was growing back. She had huge brown eyes. He knew she was his.

The priest was shouting at the old woman.

'Clean her up, please. Bring her downstairs. Here is her father. What will he think?'

She spread her hands helplessly, shouting back.

'I have no help! The nuns are always at their prayers. I can't do everything, Father!'

Pierre was watching the child. She paid no attention to the shouting. Squatting down in the filth, she began to rock backwards and forwards, her eyes fixed into the corner of the cot, as though she saw something terrible there. She began to scream again, over and over.

Pierre turned and ran from the room, his stomach heaving. He stopped on the stairway, halfway down, his face jammed into the narrow slit of the window, gasping the cool air and shaking uncontrollably. The priest came down and stood beside him, his hand on Pierre's arm.

'I am sorry. It is a shock. I understand. You see, we think she is deaf but she has no language, so we cannot tell. And there is no doctor here. We don't know why she screams. They all have such terrible memories. When the authorities come, they will take her to an asylum. But it will not be a merciful place.'

Pierre turned, once again meeting that direct blue gaze.

'How could I take care of such a child? How could I?'

'Yes, it would be difficult to do it alone.'

'And what about the other little girl?'

'If you cannot take her, she will go to an orphanage.' He hesitated. 'I promised ... they must be kept together if possible. They have no one else. If they are parted, Marie will never recover. They are like sisters. You will see.'

'I understand. But how can I look after them? I don't know anything about children. And I have no home.'

'I understand. And whatever you decide, if you take them with you, it must be done well. They have suffered enough.'

Pierre turned, and walked slowly back up the stone stairs. The door was half-open. The old woman was standing by the cot, dabbing at the mattress with a cloth. As he came into the room, she began shouting at the child, a torrent of German.

He walked over to the cot and leaned down. She was quiet now. Hesitantly, he lifted the frail little body with its bird-like bones into his arms. He rubbed his fingers over the cruel scalp, feeling the scabs. Her head was against his shoulder. Then she began screaming again; a terrible sound which went through him like pain.

The old woman was shouting in German.

'She says the child is uncontrollable. She should be put away,' the priest whispered.

Then, all at once, she was quiet. Pierre looked down. Another child was standing beside the cot, a year or two older, three or four perhaps, though it was hard to know. Her head was shaved, but dark hair was beginning to grow back in ringlets. She was singing — some other language he didn't know. Marie had closed her eyes, and was still, breathing quietly against Pierre's chest.

This, now, would be the pattern of his days.

31

Father Ruch and Pierre went several times to the convent that autumn, ferrying CARE parcels which Pierre wangled from an American liaison officer, nappies scrounged from the Red Cross, food when they could get it. There were many more children now, the nuns struggling with numbers. Aishe had begun to recognise Pierre, and she would come running out when he arrived. She called them both 'Vaati', with a generosity of spirit which was there among all the children. But Marie never came to him.

In the chaos following the end of the war, and the liberation of the camps, the two girls had not been properly registered. Father Ruch had taken them straight to the nunnery for sanctuary. It made everything more difficult. They spent some of the time between visits trying to arrange the paperwork for them. Hours spent queueing in ACC offices, endless phone calls. In the end, Pierre was helped by a kindly official in the newly reopened American consulate, who took pity on him. With Father Ruch as a witness, and Rebecca's statement that Pierre was her father, the way was opened to bring Marie back to France. It would be more difficult for Aishe.

There were thousands of orphans in Germany, children who had somehow survived the camps and those who were the victims of the Allied bombing campaigns. Corners were being cut to get the orphans to some kind of sanctuary, where they might have a good chance of life after the war, but there was still paperwork. A programme of adoption for orphans in Germany by the USA had just begun, and at least there was a system in place. But was Aishe really an orphan? Could Pierre adopt her legally? There were so few records of any of the children who had been in the camps; most had been routinely destroyed by the SS. For Aishe, there was no entry in the concentration camp records to show that she existed at all. They only had anecdotal evidence that Aishe's mother had been gassed in Auschwitz in the final days, her father months before in Belsen.

Even with Pierre's position in the Allied forces, nothing was easy. He worried about the welfare of the girls while they were at the nunnery. He gave as much money as he could spare to the Sisters, and had insisted that new, competent staff be recruited to look after all the children. He was glad now he had sold the major part of his inheritance in Brittany. That was his past, and the girls were his future. He and Father Ruch managed to have the convent raised to the status of an official refugee 'camp' for DPs. There would be more funds from other, more official, sources soon.

Marie's hair had begun to grow in red curls. She had lost that sharp nipped look on her bones, as though making up for lost time. But was still very pale, tiny for her age, and totally silent, unless wracked by screaming fits. By contrast, Aishe seemed so alive, a stocky little girl with black curls and an olive skin. Aishe talked for both of them, and though it seemed that Marie didn't hear anyone, not even her adopted sister, as Pierre watched them, he was sure she was not truly deaf.

As part of the process, they would have to take the two children into Cologne for a Medical and an assessment. Pierre dreaded having to take Marie into the city. Any tiny changes upset her and triggered screaming fits and acute distress. In the end, the new Mother Superior managed to swing a visit by a Red Cross doctor working with the unit in the area of the schloss to conduct the examination. Pierre was sure Aishe would come through with flying colours — she was a tough little girl, a survivor, in robust health, endlessly happy despite her terrible experiences, but what about Marie?

It was part of his job in Cologne, working with DPs, to record interviews with camp survivors. Their testaments were harrowing. Details had emerged from 1945 in the Nuremberg

Trials of what had happened in the camps, and the 'Doctors' Trial' was also taking place that winter, while Pierre was still working in Cologne. It chilled Pierre to the bone to think of the narrow escape of the children from an even more horrific fate at the hands of the Angel of Death.

Pierre carried Marie into the room, Aishe hanging onto his hand. Marie immediately started to scream, rigid with terror, staring past the doctor into the far corner of the room. Pierre recounted the history of both children, as much as he knew. The doctor examined Aishe first. Pierre expected both would be very underweight for their age, their growth stunted, though those months at the schloss had improved their general health. Aishe's speech development was good. With her quick mind, she had picked up German quickly, some French and English, as well as Yiddish from the Jewish orphans in the nunnery, Romany words, learned from her mother, he guessed.

'Yes. I think she must be about three, though it's hard to be specific,' the doctor said at last, laying down his stethoscope. 'Her general health is good, considering her experiences. I can't find any trace of TB. And she's speaking well. Eating well too, I should imagine.' Aishe grinned up at him. 'This one is a real survivor.'

It was Marie's turn. As gently as he could, Pierre picked her up from the corner of the room. She started to scream again. He found Aishe at his side, reaching out her hand, singing softly to her sister in that language she seemed to have invented especially for her. Marie stopped crying and was quiet.

'We have seen too many children like this. How old is she, do you think?' the doctor laid a new form in front of Pierre on the desk.

Pierre had a sudden picture of Rebecca walking through the grass towards him before he had jumped through the window. That last glimpse of her, pregnant, that morning, with the sound of the battle all around them, had never left him. Marie must have been born shortly afterwards, in the late summer of 1944, a few weeks after the D-Day landings. By the time she was born, Rebecca would have been a prisoner, transported during the fighting to one of the camps in Germany. Unbearable to think about what it must have been like, giving birth in such desperate circumstances. He remembered the woman giving birth in the rubble, his first day in Cologne.

'It's hard to be exact,' he said. 'I think she must have been born in late summer 1944, so she would be about two and a half.'

The doctor nodded and he began to examine Marie, his face grave. It wasn't easy to keep her still, although Aishe stayed in the room, holding her hand and singing to her. The doctor went back to his desk and began to make notes.

'Given the circumstances, her physical health is not as bad as I had expected. However, she is exhibiting classic symptoms of maternal deprivation. In addition, there may be a condition on the autistic spectrum. In any case, I have no doubt she is profoundly deaf — she doesn't respond in any way when I clap my hands or say her name.' He called her name again loudly. 'Marie!' She ignored him, looking once more into the corner of the room, her face impassive.

Pierre had never heard the word 'autistic', but it sounded somehow final. A sense of helplessness swept over him, and with it a longing to have Rebecca there with him in the room. As it was, he would have to cope on his own. Nothing in his training, nor in his life before, had prepared him for this. He could blow up a telephone box, a railway line, plant explosives, use time pencils, find his way through rough country in the dark. He could live in hiding for weeks, impersonate a French fishermen or a priest. But this was the toughest challenge he had ever faced, and he was lost.

'She seems to hear Aishe singing,' he said. 'I can't believe she's totally deaf. And autism — is that something she was born with? The priest, Father Ruch, told me that he doesn't remember her screaming while she was with her mother in the church. Is it because she screams, you think she's autistic?'

He shook his head, occupied with filling in sections on the form.

'No. No. I admit it's difficult to make an accurate diagnosis, and misleading to label them. But, as I said, since the end of the war, we have seen so many children like Marie. There are many unknown factors. Only in the future, we may begin to understand what has happened to them, what damage has been done to their young minds. I have just read a report by a group of doctors working with Jewish refugees. They have documented a severe lack of mental ability, the facility to build language, as well as what we call post-traumatic stress. It's shell shock, in effect; we saw it in the First World War. It relates to the trauma they have experienced. These children have been through a war — they were in the front line, in effect. They have seen more cruelty, more suffering, than any soldier could expect to have seen in his lifetime. In addition, they've lost one parent, very often both.'

He was a good man, well-intentioned. It must be hard to be a doctor in such circumstances.

He stood up, folding his stethoscope.

'What can I say to you? Perhaps you will ask me if she would be better cared for in an institution? Depending on her mental state, there are institutions which might help her. However, there are no medicines at the moment which can cure such conditions. Drugs for control perhaps, especially if she becomes violent as she grows older. You need not reproach yourself if you don't feel you could take on such a burden. But if you do decide to take her home, you will need to employ a full-time housekeeper and a nurse. It would be too difficult for a man to try to manage on his own. We men don't have the facility to look after children the way women do. However, if you have a proper arrangement in place, who knows what the future might hold.'

He shook hands with Pierre and gave him a searching look.

'We are all groping in the dark; we have never seen these kinds of conditions before. It's too early to see what will happen with any of these children. Marie may have a chance, and my diagnosis may well be inaccurate. I can only work with what I see, now, today. Whatever else, it requires love. Love may be a cure. Love, care, nurture, stability. With those factors, there is the possibility of change; even a miracle.'

'Now little Aishe!' he smiled at her as she bounced around the room, singing to herself. 'Look at her now! It does my heart good to see her. Somehow, she has come through it all unscathed. We can only hope for that for others. In any case, it's clear that the two children are very interdependent. I will mention that fact in my report, and send a copy to the authorities in Berlin.'

He shook Pierre's hand again, and watched as he retrieved Marie from her crouched position under the chair. She curled up on his shoulder. Light as a feather, easily blown away, he thought. At least now she was quiet, lying with her eyes closed. It had all been too much for her, this day. But what could he do?

The doctor scribbled on a piece of paper, and handed it to him as they left.

'There's a doctor in Paris who may be able to help Marie. I've written his address here. It could be useful. He's practising now in a small house in the 14th Arrondissement. He himself was a survivor of the camps. Now he tries to help those who must survive the peace, as well as the war.'

He shook Pierre's hand for a third time. Then, unconsciously echoing Father Ruch's words, he said 'Good luck! If you take both children, it must be done well.'

As they walked out of the room, Aishe ran back to the doctor. 'Gimme gum chum!' she shouted. The doctor looked up, startled. They heard it often in Cologne, as begging children followed the GIs through the ruined streets, but where had she heard it here? It was time to go home, away from the war.

32

The future looked bleak. Pierre didn't even know if *Le Tamaris* was still standing, and he was contemplating taking two children back there; one at least deeply traumatised, with serious mental health problems. But how could he let Marie be taken into an institution? It was unthinkable.

It had got harder every time to leave the children at the nunnery, especially now he knew more about Marie's condition. He had left more money for the care of both girls, but he had resolved, as soon as he was able, to take them home, wherever home may be.

As he drove around Cologne, he saw children everywhere, hiding in the ruins, sitting on the edges of the broken pavements, shivering in rags. Once, when he was held up by roadworks, two tiny urchins banged on the window of the car, begging for bread. A very young girl, no more than 13, leaned out of an upstairs window in one of the broken buildings. Half dressed, she beckoned to him. In that desperate city, as in all the desperate cities in war-torn Europe, he realised with a shock how vulnerable these children were. He felt exposed to it all, his eyes opened now that he had, by some extraordinary twist, two children of his own.

He was haunted by Aishe's plea to the doctor, 'Gimme gum, chum!' Now he heard it all over the city, among the half-wild children who gathered round him whenever he stopped. GIs were handing out chewing gum, even cigarettes to the older ones, probably with the best of intentions. But these children were open to exploitation, either too friendly and trusting with strangers, or, like Marie, shut down, unreachable.

It was now the winter of 1946. It would turn out to be a terrible winter across Europe. So many, weakened by war and deprivation, would die of starvation, disease or simply cold. It was hard to carry on doing his job. Each statistic which once had lain there on the page, inert, now represented living people, real suffering.

Pierre had resigned his commission, and in November his demobilisation came through. He spent his last wages on a battered Volkswagen, fur rugs, warm clothes and black market petrol. He begged more nappies, food and supplies from the Red Cross in Cologne. Then he said goodbye to Father Ruch. The priest was leaving for Berlin to help with a new group of refugees from Upper Silesia. He was Pierre's only link with Rebecca, apart from the children. He would always be grateful to him.

Before he left, Pierre begged a lift in a Liberator back to England and went back to Edward's house. Annie let him in. Edward was working for the MOD and was away in Scotland on Ministry business. It would be a long time before Pierre would be in England again. He left a letter explaining all he had not been able to say, and packed a case. His room was as he had left it, even the wheelchair in the corner.

***

Now it was time to go back to the nunnery to fetch the children. Pierre scraped hard snow from the roof of the Volkswagen where it was standing in the pound. There were Red Cross parcels to tie to the roof, and all the food he might need, a suitcase for himself and one for the girls, filled with clothes from the list which the Mother Superior had given him. Almost an afterthought, he had brought Rebecca's case from England, the folded clothes still in it. At least something of her would be brought back to *Le Tamaris*.

There was a snarl-up by the cathedral. An Army truck had skidded onto its side, blocking the road. The POWs it had been carrying were trying to right it. Snow-bulldozers and trucks

manoeuvred ponderously on the hard-packed roads, the smell
of diesel hanging in the air. It was midday before he passed
the internment camp on the outskirts of the city. The little
watchtowers wore caps of snow and he glimpsed dark streaks
of figures walking on the white ground. More loose ends of war.
Like his new daughters. Like himself.

Outside the city, it was slow going, and he began to fret. He
was anxious to get to the schloss before snow blocked the road.
It felt important to take the children home before the mountain
roads became impassable till spring.

Three days later, after a difficult journey, he left the car by
the side of the track below the nunnery. It was almost dark and
a grey weight of snow muffled the sky. Pierre hoped the car
would be safe with all their possessions inside. He would have
to risk it. He took the Red Cross parcels and the fur rug, and
skidded down the track, falling on his knees a couple of times.
He had to make two trips from the bridge to the other side,
sweating by the time he got to the top. Questions were running
through his mind. Was he doing the right thing? Would they
ever be his children? Could he ever be their father? He could
keep them warm. He could feed them. But could he love them
enough?

The children had spotted him, in the dusk, coming down the
drive. One of the nuns ran out to him and clutched his arm.

'Come. We have been waiting for you. The child Marie is
very ill.'

Pierre stopped on the gravel. A sense of Fate collecting like
dry frost in his blood. He followed the Sister into one of the
little towers, racing up the stairs, the clatter of cold stone under
his feet. Marie was in the top building, a little bed in a line of
little beds. A fire struggled in the grate.

Aishe was out of bed in a flash, grabbing his hands and
pulling him towards Marie, chattering in a mixture of Yiddish
and German. Marie was very still. Pierre reached down and

covered her with the fur rug and the rough ochre army blankets, listening to the harsh, rasping breath, feeling her hot, dry cheek. Kneeling beside her, he took her in his arms.

'She has measles. They've all had it. Even little Aishe.'

One of the nuns was standing beside him.

'Thank goodness it wasn't last winter. They're much stronger now. But it's still very bad. We have lost one already.'

'Tell me what to do,' he said.

For six days, he slept beside Marie on a camp bed. Aishe was soon running around, her few spots already healing. It was bitterly cold everywhere, but in that stone room with its sulky fire, it was colder than anywhere in the building. The nuns said the cold was a good thing. It would kill the infection.

The second night, the little boy Friti called out in terror that they were taking him away. In the morning they carried his little body out into the snow and buried him behind the chapel, in the iron hard ground, while the nuns wept.

The snow fell every night. Pierre managed to get back to the car the first day before they were totally cut off, and they had to use all the food he had kept for the journey.

Marie lay in the little room, hanging onto life, burned by the dry fever, her hands spread out childishly on the dark fur. She hardly moved, except to wake occasionally and scream. Aishe would bring her water, and sit beside her, holding her hand. Pierre cleaned her, washed her face, changed her clothes, and slept beside her every night. She belonged to him now.

On the eighth night, she was restless. Pierre didn't think her frail little body would take any more. He was afraid to pray. He stood by the window, watching the snow come down — great flakes passing the window, knowing that if he lost her, he couldn't hope any more.

It would be hard to go on.

Late in the night Pierre felt her forehead and it was cold. She was utterly still. He could hear no breathing. He went down on his knees beside her bed, on the pitted stone, and putting his head beside hers on the pillow, he wept. He didn't know how long he was there before he felt a little hand on his shoulder. It was Aishe, and behind her Sister Annunciata, who had done most to nurse the children.

'The crisis has passed. The fever has gone. She is sleeping quietly. You sleep too. Aishe and I will watch until morning.'

In the morning Pierre was woken by a touch on his arm. He sat up. Marie was leaning out of bed, looking at him. Aishe was standing beside her.

'Essen!' Aishe said firmly, watching him. When he didn't appear to respond, she shouted at the top of her voice, 'Gimme gum chum!' She drummed with her little fists on the fur rug, until the other children woke and began to cry. But Marie was laughing, not screaming.

She had been so ill, Pierre couldn't believe how well she got, so quickly. They had no more deaths. One by one the four remaining sick ones passed the crisis. The room and the staircase were noisy with convalescing children. The nuns took them out in the snow. Snow had been a terrible thing before, in the camps — a deadly enemy, bringing frostbite, death. Now for the first time it was fun. They could truly be children, and because there was warmth somewhere near, food and comfort, they waded into the snow-drifted world, growing braver every minute, crying and throwing up the white stuff, inventing snowballs, plunging forward. In everything Marie did, Pierre could see her mother, though she was timid, not brave, nor strong like Rebecca. Aishe was always by her side, giving her courage, as her own mother would have done, if she had been there.

When the snow melted at last Pierre drove back to Cologne and replenished his supplies before he returned for the children. There was that same false spring he remembered from another year. But now there was hope everywhere. Soon the real spring would begin. Marie was now almost three, still not speaking, still shut firmly in her own world, from which she would occasionally emerge, screaming. But the screaming had become less frequent. Aishe could now speak a few words of French but she still called him 'Vaati'.

He wrapped them both in the fur rugs and said goodbye to the nuns. They were busy unloading the first truckload of supplies from the Red Cross. Sister Annunciata and the Mother Superior climbed down modestly from the truck side, clutching their habits. Then a whole crowd of refugees and nuns and the Red Cross driver ferried their luggage over the swollen river and up the still snow-streaked bank on the far side, slipping and laughing, calling out messages to be remembered.

Aishe was hugely excited, trying out her languages, making the nuns laugh. The last sound he heard as they drove away was their laughter.

Pierre had told them in French about *Le Tamaris* — Aishe called it *Tamis*, and she was making up a song about it, a mixture of French, German and her familiar language Yiddish, with her favourite 'Gum Chum' repeated every couple of bars. She explained it to Marie in a private sign language they had invented.

There were floods across the road from the melting snow. The old car splashed through them, the water curving in a slow sheen, catching the sun. It made Aishe laugh again. Somehow, sometime, they might be lucky, after all.

33

Love, that sad old trickster, weaving its web. A terrible joy carried him through the ruins of Germany, along the bombed streets of forgotten towns, the smell of death and dust swept up with the wind, through the silence, subservience, past the hate, the shame, the unforgetting. Beside him, the children shone like bright talismans. They drove on, through the rubble and the burned-out camps, along minor roads when they could, hands reaching out from ruined villages. Pierre realised these were the only landscapes, the landscapes of war and ruin, the girls had ever known.

It was more terrible in France. He had not been in the north, and had seen so little of the war once the last battles began after D-Day. He had not seen how the heart of France had been ripped out, first by invasion and then by victory, as much as by defeat. For the second time in a century, her fields, farms and villages had become violent battlefields; her coastline scenes of bombardment and bloody slaughter.

They drove all night from the border, following the coast, the headlights of the car picking out cratered roads, pre-fabricated huts in the rubble, the black holes of windows in half-ruined houses, children playing on bomb sites at midnight. His own children slept, shoulder to shoulder, in the back of the car under the fur rugs.

They found no *Bienvenue,* no *Welcome Home* among the ruins, only the peeling Dubonnet signs adhering like crumbling fungus to broken walls; no accommodation, no lights, no churches with doors unbarred, no place to rest. But still the little girls slept peacefully, Marie snoring softly, her hands clutched together. Each morning, Pierre would wake at first light and drive along littered roads, looking for a safe place.

At dawn in a little town, he saw a sign: *Restaurant Perrot*. Too exhausted to go on any further, he parked the car close to the kerb, locked all the doors, wrapped himself in his jacket, and tried to sleep. He dozed and woke in fear. What was he doing, bringing the girls here, to a dying country? The force of it struck him for the first time. He had been so full of optimism. Yet, if *Le Tamaris* weren't still standing, they would be homeless. They had nothing but a car and two fur rugs, a little food, and a quantity of black market petrol coupons.

He was woken again by a woman singing in the street. The restaurant stood alone on a broken corner and in front someone, the owner perhaps, had piled the rubble from the adjoining houses into neat walls, forming a rough parking area. In front was a large notice board propped up against the wall.

ICI! Le Premier Restaurant du Nord.

Des Viandes! Des legumes! Le plat de jour!

The woman was singing as she washed the street. It had been windy in the night, and dust and rubble had come down onto the road. She was swilling soapy water in a bucket, pushing vigorously with a broom till there was a clear arc of wet.

Aishe woke and banged on the window, shouting in German.

'Stop singing, lady! You wake me up.'

The woman stopped and came back down the path towards the car. He wound down the window.

'Monsieur?' She was watching him, guarded. 'You are parking across my entrance. Please move!'

'I am sorry. It was very dark. I didn't see,' he said in French. 'Do you have a room? My daughters and I are very tired. We have come a long way.'

The woman looked puzzled. Pierre remembered the German plates on the car, a German car.

'You have come from Germany? But you are French?' There was no mistaking the tone.

'Yes, we are French. We have come a long way ... from Cologne. I have been working for the Allies. This is my daughter, Marie. And my other daughter Aishe. Do you have rooms?'

'Monsieur, pardon! I have been so inhospitable! Here, I will take the children. Don't worry, I will carry the little one. She's still sleepy!'

She pulled at the handle of the back door.

'I'm sorry! It's locked. For their safety.'

Pierre stretched back inside the car. 'Here! I'll do it, Madame.'

'Yes, you must be careful! And it is a German car. You are lucky no one threw stones at you in the night. Or worse!'

She scooped Marie into her arms.

'*Oh, ma pauvre petite lapin!*'

Stiff and sore, Pierre got out of the car.

'What you must think of me? Of course, we have rooms. And breakfast! My husband is baking. Have you read the notice? The best restaurant in the *departement*! Soon we will have three restaurants! My husband was with de Gaulle. He came over with the liberating forces. Now he has a pension and a small settlement from the General. And we have gone into business. He was a chef before the war. Lots of townspeople come out on a Sunday!'

The woman picked her way across the wet pavement, carrying Marie in her arms, Aishe skipping behind. Pierre waited for Marie to start screaming, but she was quiet.

It had begun to rain. The street was very quiet. Pierre dropped the cases on the pavement and leaned on the roof of the car. It was dusty and tacky now. While they had slept, someone had scrawled 'Filthy Schleuh' above the windscreen. The woman was right. They had been lucky not to have been stoned. Or worse. He knew it was because of the car, but still he couldn't push away the loneliness which had been there since they crossed the border into France. A sense of alienation, worse because of the children. Perhaps they didn't belong here after all.

He carried the cases through the open door of the restaurant. There was a smell of coffee, real coffee, new-baked bread. Marie was sitting on the woman's lap, with Aishe beside her. There were small tables and a large central one. A huge man with bare forearms sat eating his breakfast in a white apron. Croissants on a checked cloth. A young girl came in from the doorway on the far side of the room, a jug in either hand. She looked at him and smiled.

The older woman stood up, with Marie in her arms.

'Sit yourself down. Hot milk for the little one. Goat's milk. So good for babies! We have two goats now. Milk is so hard to come by and the *laitier* is unreliable. We reared our own boy on goat's milk. Ah, he was fine, wasn't he, François? A fine boy!'

'Does he help you here, in the restaurant?'

'No, no.' The woman shook her head.

'He's gone. Our only son. It was a terrible sorrow. And I had to bear it alone, my husband having left, you see, to be with the Free French. He was such a brave boy too. In the Résistance! In the *maquis* over to the south, so they say. But it doesn't do to talk too much about it. Le General disapproves of the *maquis*! They went a little wild after the Liberation.'

'Now, Mother, serve the milk,' the man said. 'Your guests have come a long way.'

'Yes, I have been serving with the Allies in Germany.'

Pierre took a sip of scalding coffee, trying to fend off a deep weariness.

'Forgive me,' the man said. 'Your accent is a strange one. A little like the English, a little like Breton.'

'I was from Brittany, yes, then I lived in England for a while. Now we're going home, to our farm, near the sea at Sainte Croix.'

'In the *bocage*!' the man whistled through his teeth. 'Let's hope you find something to go home to! There was terrible fighting around Sainte Croix. Terrible.'

The woman laid her hand on his arm.

'Now, François. Don't worry the poor man. Let him eat his breakfast. I have a wonderful room for you, Monsieur. And just the thing for the baby! A wooden cot my son slept in till he was five. I'll show you. Why don't you come up when you have finished your breakfast? That other little one is such a lively thing! Look at her running about! You won't get her to go to sleep. I'll take them with me into the washhouse. They can help me. Then you can sleep. You look as though you haven't slept for days. And your leg! You're injured! And your poor face! I couldn't help noticing.'

'An accident. A long time ago. I'm almost better now.'

His eyes seemed to be closing. He couldn't fight it any longer, his speech thick, far away.

Pierre followed her up the wooden stairs, into a cool room with a double bed. She closed the shutters, leaving just a thin bar of light across the coverlet. The door closed softly. He could hear Aishe running about downstairs. Marie was not screaming. They would be safe for now.

'Perhaps we will find a home, somewhere,' he thought. He was asleep before he could feel any more.

34

By some miracle he had found a place where they could be safe for a little while. Colette, Madame Perrot, and her husband and daughter were kind and hospitable, glad of his custom. Glad of their company too, especially the children. The little restaurant was doing well. It was always busy, but to Pierre's amazement Marie seemed to settle, not minding the strangers. Only occasionally would they hear that terrible screaming, but somehow Colette soothed her in a way Pierre never could. Aishe was in her element, helping out in the kitchen and getting under everyone's feet. It almost felt like being in a family. Pierre too began to feel less like a stranger in France.

They were only 50 miles from *Le Tamaris*. Pierre thought the girls would be safe with Colette while he went back to the farm to reconnoitre. He needed to know if there was still a house to live in. He dreaded what he might find.

He left the Restaurant Perrot in the early morning, its shutters still closed, the children sleeping. Pierre had explained he would be away for a few days, and he would come back for them. Used to his comings and goings from their time in the orphanage, now happy and secure at the restaurant, they accepted his going away without question.

Spring wasn't far away, and somehow everything seemed more hopeful. He drove along the little roads, carefully avoiding the craters. There had been heavy fighting around the villages of the *bocage* and he knew the port at Sainte Croix had been badly hit. He hardly recognised it as he drove through. The main square had been cleared and, where there had been houses crowding in, many of them had just disappeared, or were piles of rubble and broken beams. Workmen were pulling down the rest of the three-story buildings and rebuilding further back. To his surprise, however, the quayside was crowded with market stalls. Pierre found himself looking for Paul and Armand as he drove through. The memories he had dreaded began to flood back. For months now he had pushed them away, focusing entirely on the children and their survival. Now he had to face them.

Pierre stopped the car on the little headland and looked out over the sea. It was a perfect spring morning, the grass green again, wild carrot and sea plants on the cliff. He saw the remains of the gun emplacement below, the wire still in place, though softened by tamarisk bushes which clung to the cliff in the salt air.

He drove the car on, slowly now, fearful of what he might find. When he came to the small crossroads, he stopped the car and got out. It had been raining in the night. A stream had overflowed onto the road; water catching fire in the morning sun. There was a clear blue sky, birdsong, iridescence on new leaves.

In a little while, he would find what ruins remained of *Le Tamaris*. This is where he would begin, however difficult it was. This was their future. It was all they had left, the three of them, and he would make it work. With his bare hands, if necessary.

Foolishly, he wanted to come back in the way he had the first time. Leaving the car, he fought his way up the track, scratched by vicious brambles.

He tripped against something hard, the rusting remains of a bicycle. It was further than he remembered. Then he broke out into the deserted yard. A tangled mass of dead trees and bushes half-buried in mud, smashed to the ground by deep tank tracks which had circled the farmhouse, footprints of a predator on the prowl. Some deadly encounter between the Allies and an enemy in retreat. The skeleton of a cow lay rib-deep in the pond. There were more tank tracks fossilised in the mud, the marks of fire all around the yard. Two of the farm buildings had been destroyed — there must have been a fierce battle in one corner, a flame thrower from a tank had blackened the ruined walls of the granière. In the byre, two walls had been blown in by a powerful blast. Miraculously though, the farmhouse itself seemed largely untouched by the battle, though a large part of the roof had fallen in.

He skirted the pond, memories leaping at him. Thomas dying in the road, the stutter of the guns; the first time Pierre had seen Rebecca by the pump. It was still standing, rusty, lichen growing on the handle, a nest inside the broken head. It had been a long time. Now this was his; his to rebuild.

He walked across the yard. Two bullets were embedded in the door. It was ajar. He ducked his head and walked into the dark.

It was all there, as he had seen it in his dream. The kitchen with years of mould in the pots, the range covered in chicken droppings, an empty bottle of marc on the table. Thomas's chair, against the window. A fragment of net, and a cork float which rats had gnawed.

Green darkness filtered through the window; ivy and giant dock blocked the light. It was hopeless to bring children here, to try to put it back together. Too late to begin again.

He climbed the stairs into the little room where he had slept under the eaves. It was open to the sky, mouldy wallpaper still clinging to the wall, broken tiles from the hole in the roof. He was drawn to the window and, looking down, saw the yard in all its decay; all four fields, rank with nettles, stretching up to the line of the hedge. What a thing to fight for. A humble piece of France, a dead cow in the centre of the pond.

Pierre clattered down the stairs and out of the door into the yard, picking his way through the mud towards the barn. Inside there was a sweet smell of hay. The last time it was gathered would have been while he was still in England. Then he had not even met Rebecca.

He picked up a handful of the hay and buried his nose in it. It had lasted well. Grass was growing on it now, but that sweet tobacco smell was still there. He could feed his animals. He could have a living cow in the byre. Even a goat. The children could drink the milk and grow strong. He could mend the pump, and they would have good water from the well. Jacques might come up from the village and help him to restore the buildings, if he were still alive. Anyway, someone would come; he would find someone. Somehow, he would mend enough of the roof to make the rest of the house habitable. He could rebuild the byre. He could put pigs into the fields for winter. There was a great shortage of meat.

They would have a place of their own.

For three days, he laboured to clear a space in the kitchen. From some of the broken beams, he created a little bedroom space near the range, where the children would be warm at night. Then he lit the range. It smoked badly, sending him coughing into the yard. When he crawled onto the remains of the roof, he found a jackdaw's nest in the chimney and cleared it out, much to the fury of the female bird, who was sitting on eggs. After that the fire burned sweetly, and soon the kitchen was full of warmth, coming alive again.

The pump was bunged up with rust, but he cleaned it out with an old brush he found in the yard, and very soon the water flowed cold and clear. So they would have water, food and shelter.

It was time to bring the children home. They said goodbye to Mme Perrot and her husband. They would be their first guests once he got the place straight, part of their family now.

Aishe sang all the way.

35

The first fragile breath of Normandy spring. Spears of fat bluebells, a frog chorus in the little river beyond the field. The banks of the *bocage* starred with stitchwort, celandine, clotted clumps of primrose and early purple orchids. Pierre remembered his mother, on their occasional outings together, naming the wild flowers, freed from the spell of the dark house, away from the iron disapproval of his grandmother.

Now he was making a home in France for his own children — one of them a broken, silent child, with her terrible unspoken memories of the loss of her mother. What had it done to her? Father Ruch had told him that Rebecca was taken from her children in the church, mercifully not raped in front of them. Marie had screamed then. Though largely silent, she was screaming still.

And there was Aishe, always singing. She had been less than three when her mother had left her for the gas chamber, the child hidden in darkness under the hut, fed bread by the women from their meagre rations, a chick in a nest of huddled, terrified, feral children. Where had that inexhaustible singing come from? Father Ruch had said it was a gift from God; if there were a God. The lightness of being which radiated from her, laughter, the gift of spontaneous joy. It was a light for Marie in her darkness. For Pierre too, Aishe was a gift from Rebecca, across the silence.

That summer he worked. As soon as he had partially fixed the roof, he slept every night in his old bedroom. The children slept by the range, kept in all night. It was still cold in early spring — often a frost on the cobbles. And there was another presence in the kitchen. When they had arrived back at *Le Tamaris* together, an old dog was sitting in the yard, gnawing a cow bone. Pierre had buried the cow in the back field, not wanting to distress the children when they arrived home. The dog had found it.

There had been a dog at the nunnery, a German Shepherd, who had taken up residence there and was fed on scraps. Now it was Marie who went towards the stray first. Pierre tried to stop her but as usual she ignored him, and when he tried to hold her back, she struggled out of his arms. He was worried. There were so many stray dogs in the ruined villages, and rabies was rife. But this dog was gentle and quiet, standing passively while she put her hand on his head and stroked him. He was big, some kind of lurcher perhaps, who looked as though his mother had been crossed with a giant poodle. After a few days, Pierre discovered Marie feeding him bits of her food, completely at home with him in her silent way. They seemed to share an understanding. It was Aishe who named him Petsha. From that first day, Petsha took over their lives, taking charge of the farm. It was entirely his place, and the children were his to protect. Pierre never needed to worry when he was in the fields. If they went too near water, he would stand in front of them, blocking their path. If strangers came to the farm, he gave an impressive display of aggression. His coming was a gift, but most important of all, he and Marie shared an extraordinary rapport. She calmed down immediately, and the screaming stopped. Sometimes Pierre would hear her muttering to the dog — the first time they had heard any speech from her.

At the end of the first week, they went to the local market. Pierre asked around, but no one seemed to own the dog. He was a victim of war as much as they were. Pierre noticed that if there was any bit of cloth hanging on a chair, he would drag it down to the floor and curl up on it — a little comfort in what must have been a comfortless world.

While he was at the market, Pierre bought a goat with a kid from an old farmer, and half a dozen geese. He had rescued the *gazo* from the barn and got it started. With Aishe and Marie jammed into the front, they managed to get the goat and the geese home without incident. As soon as he unloaded them from the truck, the dog appeared, lying flat on the ground, herding the goat and kid into the byre, as though he had been doing it all his life. He probably had. He must have been a good dog for someone. The children were delighted. A few days later, Pierre came down in the morning to find Petsha had somehow got into the house — he suspected Marie had let him in — and he was curled up in front of their makeshift bedroom. From then on, that was where he slept.

Pierre began the repairs to the farm, starting before dawn and working till long after dark. Then he would carry the children in his arms, often sleepy after a day in the sun, and put them to bed with the fur rugs over them.

Edward had used his MOD contacts to send Pierre's piano over from England, promising to come himself as soon as he could. Pierre had trouble persuading him in his letters that the house and farm was still ruined. It would be better for him to wait a while. He was excited to hear he was a step-grandfather. It seemed to have given him a new lease of life.

The piano had pride of place in the corner by the range. It was a little out of tune after its journey, but from then on Pierre played in the evening, by candlelight, as the children lay in their beds. They seemed to find it a comfort and Aishe always asked him to play before they went to sleep. This was one of the ways that he realised Marie was not really deaf — she always listened with great attention, sometimes humming the melody softly to herself after he finished. One night when Pierre was upstairs in bed, sure that they were safely asleep, he was startled to hear notes played hesitantly on the piano. He tiptoed downstairs. Moonlight was flooding the kitchen. Marie was standing by the piano in her old Red Cross pyjamas, absorbed, picking out a tune he had played for them earlier that evening. Next day, he began to teach them both. Aishe wasn't interested, and quickly gave up, though she had a fine voice and loved to sing. But Marie, still silent, was totally absorbed and quickly made progress. It was as though she too had found her voice.

Although Pierre had avoided Sainte Croix as much as possible, word about their homecoming had got around. One morning, as he was carrying a pail of goat's milk into the house, the children came running up the track, Aishe shouting that someone was coming. He recognised Madeleine, thinner and older, with two small children. She was followed by Genier, thinner too, bent almost double under a load.

Genier had a haunted look. He had been imprisoned in the camps. Madeleine had survived, though the Nazis had taken reprisals for Resistance activity nearby. Robert and two other young men had been shot in front of the whole village outside the church. Madeleine had been pregnant with their second child.

They brought food and wine, little cakes that Madeleine had baked for the children, fruit, almost unobtainable after the war, even a little chocolate. Aishe danced around them at the kitchen table, excited to have visitors, but Marie hid behind the door, refusing to come into the room.

'A feast to welcome you home, you and your new family!' said Genier, tears in his eyes, standing up to make a toast. They had heard about the children. Everyone seemed to know their history.

Paul had also come back from the camps. He had lost an arm and grown old, but he was glad of work, and came to help Pierre the next day. Madeleine came most mornings, walking up from the village, or on her bicycle with her children balanced on the crossbar. She would cook for them all, and it meant Pierre could spend more time on the building work or in the fields, without worrying about feeding the children. Marie grew braver, and she and Aishe took to the other two children — a boy who looked just like Robert and named after him, born after his father had died, and a girl of four, little Odile.

Marie was at last beginning to make some noises, though no one could understand her. Pierre was increasingly sure she wasn't even partially deaf. He had written to the doctor in the 14th Arrondissement who had been recommended by the Red Cross, and he had agreed to see Marie. He had been working with children in Paris who were returning from the camps. One day Pierre took the train to Paris with Marie, leaving Aishe with Madeleine.

The doctor met them at the door of his consulting rooms above a *boulangerie* in Montparnasse.

'I must apologise for these cramped quarters! My house was taken from me by the Germans during the Occupation. It was a beautiful house! Alas, they took everything. Now, after the war, I must begin again!'

He squatted down in front of Marie.

'So! This is the little girl!'

Marie hung back. Pierre waited for the screaming to begin, but she was looking at the doctor curiously.

He listened carefully to everything Pierre told him, and then examined Marie. She was very quiet and Pierre realised how far she had come already since her days in the orphanage.

'So! After my examination, I do not think this child is autistic. That was a common misdiagnosis amongst doctors after the war. And as you yourself have perceived, she is not deaf. You see, no one had seen children like this before, children who had survived the conditions in the camps. The nearest I can explain to you was the shell shock suffered by soldiers in the First World War. I have now seen many children in the same state. They are being sent to me by doctors from all the Occupied countries. Especially those children, those few tragic children, who survived the camps. I believe she is not deaf, but suffering from severe post-traumatic stress and acute maternal deprivation. Therapy would be difficult as she has no language to express her pain. My prescription, my medicine, is a return to normal life, with love and security. This could well bring about a miraculous change. However, we must wait. We must be patient.'

Paris was beautiful that day — summer trees, an air of gaiety and hope, even though poverty was all around. Pierre felt truly hopeful for the first time. The doctor had suggested that he find a piano teacher for Marie. It was a way she might find to express herself.

'Language will come more slowly' he had said. 'Music will be her language. You will see!'

It was a long journey home on the train. Marie slept peacefully on his shoulder. He was glad to get back to the farm. It felt like coming home. Madeleine had cooked a meal for them, the kitchen was warm and welcoming, and Aishe climbed onto his lap to hug him.

Pierre was aware that Madeleine had hopes for them — in many ways it was a perfect solution for the four children. But he held back. Perhaps he would always be in love with Rebecca, a part of him hoping that one day she would come home, but he knew too it was only a foolish dream.

He tried to explain some of this to Madeleine, not wanting her to have any expectation that their relationship could develop. It was difficult. There had been nothing spoken between them, but she understood. She was a warm, lovely woman, with a generous heart. He wished he could have loved her in return.

At night he would light the lamp and sit at the wooden table by the smoky range. It was lonely but he was glad to be tired, glad to be bone weary, glad of the aching muscles in his damaged legs. Sleep was a benediction.

And now, Pierre realised, he had never really known *Le Tamaris* in the summer — in those long Normandy summers when the hedges were full of late flowers and orchids. All he had ever known of Rebecca's farm was the war, fear, sadness and loss. He had never known its gifts — the gifts the countryside gave back, the slow return of happiness, restoration, affirmation of life. Until that spring when he had brought back the little girls, frightened birds, to some kind of sanctuary. He watched the land begin to heal them too.

36

The summer passed. The big field was cut for hay. It was pretty poor stuff but next year would be better. Pierre had mended the hay cart and they bought an old horse to pull it. The children lay in the back as they brought the last load into the barn. Aishe was singing, looking up at the stars. By the time he got into the yard they were both asleep.

The rest of the land in Brittany was eventually sold. With the money Pierre bought more hectares on the derelict farms around, and began to put up new buildings. Marie and Aishe grew stronger, more content.

One morning in September, while he was repairing a corner of the barn, he found a small hiding place. It was full of papers — torn from an exercise book, and covered in sketches of the Atlantic Wall. He remembered Rebecca's 'passport' to England — the passport she had never needed in the end.

There had been no news of Rebecca since early June, when a letter from London had confirmed she was 'untraceable'. The Soviets had 'no record of her presence in the Eastern Zone'. There was only *Le Tamaris* and the children to believe in now.

The nights grew longer. Pierre whitewashed the kitchen and put in a new floor and windows. He still kept the old range and Thomas's table. They had many visitors. Everyone knew the story of the children now. Survivors came at weekends to help rebuild the farm, though most of the *maquisards* he had known were dead. Philippe's group had almost all been shot in the raid or had died in the camps, and Jean had been executed. A few had got away, they said, but it wasn't too healthy nowadays to admit to having been a *maquisard*. It reeked too much of anarchy and communism — and although the communists were still strong, central government was clamping down on all private armies. Pierre heard that one or two joined the Foreign Legion. Others, who couldn't settle, turned to crime. The 'best days' of the young men were over. He heard on the grapevine that Bernard and Antoine had escaped to another group of *maquis* after the battle at the château, but had been sent eventually to the camps in the last days of the war.

France was desperately poor, and had missed out on war reparations which were being poured into Germany. It was an attempt by the Allies to avoid a repeat of the conditions after the first war, which had enabled Hitler to rise to power, but it caused much bitterness. Edward wrote that Britain was in the same desperate position as they were in France. There was strict rationing he said. They were better off in the French countryside than Edward in his mansion flat in the centre of London. He wrote that it was worse than in the war, apart from the bombing. Queuing for everything. Fuel was short, and few had enough food. Pierre was glad of the goat's milk, and the gifts from people in the village. They brought provisions, sometimes even clothes, for the children.

Genier got into the habit of arriving just as Pierre was going to bed, yarning half the night if he could. His eyes never lost that haunted look.

'I'm trying to start up another *alimentation* in the village,' he said one night, arriving late and accepting a glass of marc. 'What do you think? Though supplies are hard to come by, and money is short, of course!'

Pierre refilled his glass, trying to fend off tiredness, knowing how much the old man needed to talk.

'I'd be happy to give you a loan, if you would take it?'

Genier shook his head.

'No. Thank you. You're a good friend but I'll manage. You'll see, in a year or two, I'll be a rich man!'

'I should be able to kill a pig soon,' Pierre said. 'I hope you won't refuse some of my pork! Anyway, I want to share it with the village. They have been kind to us, with all the gifts they leave.'

'Of course!' Genier nodded, draining his glass, and standing up. 'I must go. I can see you're tired. It is good of you to listen to me and all my ramblings. The village know how hard you work for the two little girls. However short of food they are, they will always help you. Our children are the future of France. By the way, are you sure all the gifts come from the village itself?'

'What do you mean?'

'You've been so busy in the fields getting the drainage in, you may not have noticed. Did you know there's a Romani family camping with their caravan in the copse at the far end of your land? They've been there a few days. The word in the village is that they have been leaving gifts for you at your gate. No idea why.'

The next morning, he took Petsha, and leaving the children with Madeleine, he went up to the little wood at the far end of their land. But there was nothing there, only a small patch of burned earth, and some wheel tracks in the mud.

A few days later, when Pierre brought the children into the yard, after they had helped him in the fields, a man was sitting outside the door. Dark, with long black hair. Pierre knew at once he was Romany.

The man stood up and bowed.

'Forgive my intrusion,' he said. 'I am Aishe's uncle. I am called Harman. The brother of her mother. The only one of the family to survive the camps.'

Pierre looked down at Aishe. She was hanging back, puzzled. He struggled with conflicting emotions.

'You are welcome. Please come in. Have some food with us.'

He shook his head. 'My people wish to thank you for all you have done for Aishe. You saved our child, and we have watched how you have taken care of her. We wish to offer to bring her back into our family, if the burden is too much.'

Pierre looked down at Aishe. She was singing to herself, one of her little songs, her arm entwined with Marie's.

'She is one of our family too,' Pierre said at last. 'She is precious to us. We wouldn't want to lose her. Marie's mother gave her to Rebecca when she knew she was going to die, to look after her as her own. Now Rebecca has gone ... I have adopted her.'

'We understand. You have done well to save her. Although we are travelling people, many now understand the value of education, a settled life. But if she is to stay here, we would wish her to know something of her own people. We would like to come sometimes. With your permission, perhaps we may teach her something of her heritage.'

'You will always be welcome. It will be a wonderful thing for Aishe to learn about her people.'

'That is good. And in the meantime, I have brought her a gift, from the *sithi* in the east. We call it a *cimbalom*. A kind of zither. You will not know that Aishe's mother was a great singer of Romany songs, the songs of our people. Sometimes, when I have come close to the farm, I have heard Aishe singing too. We would like to help her continue the tradition of her mother. This *cimbalom* was designed for her. It is light and small, made specially for a child.'

A package, wrapped in sacking, was leaning against the doorway. Squatting down and unwrapping it, he held it out to Aishe.

'Come, Aishe.'

She danced forward, still singing, full of confidence as ever.

'This is from your mother, child,' he said in French. 'You will always be one of our people. It is for you to continue her heritage. We will come sometimes to tell you about her.'

Aishe put one finger out and plucked one of the strings. A strange, almost unearthly sound echoed across the yard.

'Shiny! Nice!' she laughed, delighted.

Harman looked at Pierre, dark eyes in a dark face.

'Our family were the great singers of the north. We were famous, I too am a singer. If Aishe is to stay with you, we would like to teach her some of the great songs of our travelling people. And we would like to teach her to play the *cimbalom*. For her mother's sake, you understand.'

He wouldn't stay, although Pierre tried to persuade him to eat with them. His caravan was on the road, he said, and they had a long journey before them.

'I'll come back sometimes, if I may. I can see she is well and healthy, and settled here. It is a blessing. Our people have suffered a great deal. Very little is known as yet, but it was terrible for our people, this war. Many of us were killed in the gas chambers. All I ask is that she doesn't forget her other family. For her mother's sake. Then I am happy.'

They walked with him to the gate, Aishe still singing, dancing ahead of them.

He smiled down at her.

'She has her mother's gift. She will be a great singer one day!'

He reached out and shook Pierre's hand.

'Thank you! We are forever in your debt. And remember, all is not lost. It may be that Marie's mother lives too! I have the Sight and I am sure of it.'

37

Sometimes the farm was visited by vagrants who trailed the slow length of France, desperate refugees looking for work, searching for a home. Pierre saw in their faces something he had felt, that desperate hunger for a place which had driven DPs in Cologne to suicide, and which, at last, had brought him to *Le Tamaris*. He would offer those wanderers shelter, for a few days or for as long as they needed, but one morning they would be gone, forcing exhausted bodies down the long road towards the sun, perhaps to die at last in a ditch, without friends.

The first morning of the frost, Pierre was finishing off the plastering in the children's new bedroom, when Marie appeared at the door.

'What is it, Marie?'

She was silent as ever, but grasped him by the hand and pulled him down the stairs, tugging him out into the yard.

'Mama!' Her first word! 'Mama!' More urgent.

'No, Marie. I'm sorry. Mama isn't coming. Not today!'

He bent down and picked her up, holding her on his shoulder. She twisted round to look at him.

'Mama!' There was no one there.

He held her tight, close to tears.

'Maybe she will come, one day!'

Marie nodded, pointing at the gate.

Aishe came running out of the house.

'I can see her, Papa! I know she is coming.'

'Mama!' Marie slid down from his arms and ran to the gate.

'Mama!'

He began to make breakfast for the girls, croissants Madeleine had baked for them the day before. Hot milk from the goat, little tasks comforting him. He was shaken by emotion, by the sense of loss, feeling it again through the children, as he had on so many lonely nights.

It was a dream. She would never come.

The next day at dawn while the children slept, Pierre saw an old woman walking slowly through the gateway. He stood in the doorway of the barn, afraid to show himself in case she might be frightened away. Often these wanderers would root along the hedge for eggs, or would beg for water. He could not begrudge them anything. It was a lonely road through the *bocage* and only a few were going home.

The woman drew nearer. He saw, in the first red light, that her feet were bare. She reached the pump, her hands going out to it, to the cold iron. She lifted up her face to the sky, it seemed in a gesture of despair.

She stood there a long time while he watched. Then she leaned forward and threw her whole weight on the pump. The water sprang scarlet in the dawn light over her bare feet.

Leaving the shadow of the barn, Pierre began to walk forward. Uncertain. Her face turned towards him. For a moment, he saw it all there — the tracks of tanks, dead faces in the snow, the slow dying. He saw it all.

It was her face.

38

That first evening, she disappeared. When Pierre searched frantically through the yard and the ruined buildings, he found her already asleep, an exhausted, unconscious sleep, in the hay barn amongst the old bales. Petsha curled up beside her.

For a long time, she seemed to inhabit some shade, some terrible place, beyond their reach. Pierre wasn't sure she even truly recognised him or the children. It was hard for them all, especially Marie and Aishe. She seemed to look through them into another place, as though some other script were running in her head, a continuous film on a loop, and they were only shadows.

It was late spring now, but would it have made any difference if it were winter? In the daytime she would sit in the yard under the blackened shells of the tamarisk trees, staring in front of her into some unimaginable distance. For several weeks she stayed there, sleeping most of the time, not speaking. By the end of the first week a parcel had been left by the gate, with clothes and boots for her. Not new of course — there were no new clothes to be had — but serviceable, and they fitted. Someone must have seen her walking the roads on her way to *Le Tamaris*, her feet bare, her clothes hanging in strips. And sometime after, she must have bathed in the river, because the day after he had left the bag for her, she was wearing the new clothes and she smelt good again. A long time after, when he was digging out a new floor in the granière, he found she had buried her old clothes under a pile of stones.

After that first day, she never ate in the house, but would squat outside under the dead tamarisk trees. The children watched her quietly, never going to her. Only on that first morning, Marie had gone to her, touching her skirt, Aishe behind her, more hesitant. But now they seemed to understand that although she was with them, in some strange way she was not there at all.

In those first weeks, she would only come into the house very briefly, for a few minutes at a time, a frightened animal at the table, ready to take flight as she tore at her bread, slurping a few mouthfuls of soup. Then she would run outside again. But gradually, gradually, Pierre could see she was beginning to wake from the nightmare world she was inhabiting. He found her one afternoon, sitting in the sunshine, the dog beside her, touching each of the children's faces. It was as though she couldn't believe they were there, in front of her. After that, she clung to them desperately, holding their hands and dragging them around the yard with her. At first it was fun, and they laughed, but after that they began to avoid her. It hurt Pierre to see her like that, and to see the children had begun to run from her, afraid. Marie was still almost mute. She had never spoken the word 'Mama' again.

Pierre had begun to rebuild the hay barn in time for the harvest, but it wasn't really in a safe state. One morning he woke to hear a crash, and running outside half-asleep, he saw that the end part of the barn, where she was sleeping, had collapsed. He began to throw the heavy rubble out of the way like a madman, sobbing. But some instinct, which perhaps had enabled her to survive, had prompted her move upstairs into the loft the night before. Pierre found her there at last, asleep in the hay, the dog beside her. He couldn't help himself. He put his arms around her for the first time since the day she had arrived — when she had pushed him away with such violence he had almost fallen. This time she just lay there, passive against him, neither moving away nor responding. Somehow it was worse.

That morning Pierre began to build a shelter for her under the tamarisk trees. Miraculously, the blackened, burned stumps were full of spring growth. He knew how much she had always loved those trees, how she used to sit under them on a stool, preparing vegetables or plucking a thin chicken. It was so dark in the kitchen, she said, and she liked to be outside in the light. It made her happy. Pierre remembered the photographs he had seen of the huts in the concentration camps. How had she endured that terrible darkness?

He finished the shelter in a day. It was only a rough thing. It was impossible to get new wood. He used the old beams from the ruined buildings, dragging them across the yard, and pinning them with iron nails from the roof timbers. He bent over some of the growing branches of the tamarisk trees, and found an old tarpaulin at the back of the cowshed to make it waterproof. The children loved it immediately, as children love playhouses. Aishe christened it *p'tit maison*, and made Pierre write the words in charcoal on the beam. The dog went in immediately and then the children. Reluctantly Rebecca followed. It was a great success. From then on, whenever possible, the children insisted on having their meals outside on the cobbles. Pierre laid straw bales for them and brought them bowls of soup and the *andouiette* which Madeleine gave them from her father's *boucherie*, which they had hung on a beam to dry in the kitchen. That first day of the *p'tit maison*, they all sat down together, using the bales as the table. It was like a game. The children thought it was a wonderful picnic. Pierre wondered what would happen when it rained. But, for the first time, he saw Rebecca smile.

That night the children went missing from their beds in the kitchen, and when he went outside to look for them, the whole family were asleep in the shelter, wrapped in each other's arms. His little family. Pierre went to his own room. He had still never got round to finishing his bedroom and it was half-open to the sky. He lay awake, filled with a strange mixture of gratitude and loneliness, listening to their voices, hearing her speak for the first time.

There were often parcels of food by the farm gate, but with the sensitivity the village had always shown, no one but Paul visited in those first weeks. It was as though they understood they needed a quiet time together. After all, so many of them had been through the same experience. Pierre felt bad about Madeleine. He had used her kindness, and the children missed their playmates. He just hoped she understood.

Paul came back to help him in the fields, and in the rebuilding of the farm, but he never came to the house. He brought his own bread, which he ate down by the river. Pierre was grateful to have that space for Rebecca.

On impulse, for her birthday, which he had remembered, he bought her an old horse in Sainte Croix, a quiet mare, sensitive, from a friend of his, Jacques Anniac who dealt in horses. The children made her a card. The horse was to be a present from them all. She seemed pleased, and ransacked the attic rooms, mercifully still unlooted, and found a saddle and bridle. She took off that evening, and was gone for hours, coming back with the horse sweating. Pierre rubbed the mare down and bedded her in the old stable. The next evening, it was the same. And every night, he was afraid she would never come back again.

She was still shut down, though she talked to the horse and to Petsha, and sometimes to the children. But Pierre couldn't reach her. She barely spoke to him, and nothing of the past. Those terrible years lay between them like a great river, uncrossable. He could not begin the conversation and neither could she. Sometimes in the evenings he would play the piano in the kitchen with the door open, and Marie would come, and play her tunes with him, the ones she was learning with the village teacher, while Aishe sang her made-up songs, plucking at the strings of the *cimbalom*. One evening, he looked up to see her standing in the doorway. By this time the children were no longer afraid of her. They ran to her, dragging her to the piano.

Pierre heard Marie whisper *Mama!* Her first and still her only word.

He had made a proper bedroom for the children; re-roofed it, painted the walls with limewash and he found some second-hand toys and pictures in the *marché* in Sainte Croix. Somewhere in the back streets on a stall, Aishe had found a flamenco doll which slept with her. Marie, the silent child, had bought a trumpet in the *bricolage* which she played endlessly, driving him mad, as she tooted it around the yard. Gradually, they began to sleep in the new place, and he would sit downstairs until they were asleep, tiptoeing up to make sure they were safe. But Rebecca still slept in her place in the yard.

Quietly, one summer dusk, Genier appeared, clutching a bottle of *eau de vie* and carrying a great pie in a metal dish. Pierre was struck by how thin he was, still — he never seemed to put on any weight — and there was that heavy sadness about him which didn't go with how he remembered him. Genier sat down beside Rebecca in the yard, on one of the straw bales, and enveloped her in one of his great hugs — he was still an expansive man despite his thinness. Pierre went to find glasses and mugs, and they toasted each other silently. Then they sat in the yard and ate the pie Pierre had heated in the stove.

'This is a gift from the late Madame Genier!' he said, raising his tin mug. 'She taught me how to make it, and I have cooked it myself, in honour of Rebecca's return!'

One morning, when Pierre was struggling to get the *gazo* going — there still wasn't much diesel for transport, and he had long ago run out of black market fuel — he turned to see she was standing on the corner of the shed, watching. She had still hardly spoken to him, all those months, just politeness, 'please' and 'thank you', always grateful.

He stopped, wiping his hands on an oily rag.

'Are you alright?' she said.

'Yes. Thank you.'

There was a pause. He could hear the children laughing in the yard, playing tag; Marie tootling on her trumpet.

'How did you find the children?' she asked at last, in a half-whisper. 'It seems like a miracle you found them, after everything.'

It was the longest sentence she had spoken to him since her return.

'It was Father Ruch. He came to me when I was working in Cologne. He brought your note with him, and told me what had happened. We drove to the orphanage where he had left the children for safety. Then I adopted them, brought them here. It seemed the right thing to do.'

'Marie doesn't speak. What's wrong with her? She never seemed to hear, even when she was a baby ... I remember. Is that why, because she's deaf?'

'I took her to a doctor in Paris. He was recommended to me by the Red Cross. He says she isn't deaf. It's just ... what happened to her. A lot of children are like that, the doctor said. Marie speaks a little sometimes now, just noises, but I can understand. She used to scream all the time. Then you came and she spoke her first word!'

'Yes, I will never forget. Mama!'

She turned away, looking into the sunlit yard where the children were playing. Then she turned back.

'It must have been difficult for you. Thank you.'

'They are my children too.'

'Of course. Yes.'

There was a pause.

'Do we have any money? I've been worrying.'

'We have enough to live on, before I start selling the pigs, farming the land properly. I've made a plan. We can talk about it. See what you think.'

'Oh. I see. You have a plan. Oh! I would like to start fishing again sometime. I suppose my boat has gone. I don't know … I always loved the sea … I used to run the farm by myself, remember.'

'You don't have to worry about anything. I will always take care of you, and the children.'

She was silent, scraping at the cobbles with her foot.

'I would like to talk to you,' she said. 'Could I come into the kitchen this evening?'

'Of course. It's your kitchen too.' He swallowed. Perhaps this wasn't the right thing to say, the right time. 'I miss you in the evenings. Now the children are sleeping in the house, it would be nice…'

She gave a little shake, as though getting rid of something.

'I'm being very selfish, but it's hard for me. I don't expect you to understand. But I do need to talk to you. I'll come this evening.'

'I'll make us some food. We can eat together.' Pierre saw she was hesitating. 'It doesn't have to be much. We can talk and eat.'

That evening, she came in quietly as Pierre was sitting at the table, preparing a *petit salade*. Someone had left a bottle of wine at the bottom of the lane. He poured a glass for each of them with the only two glasses he owned, picked up second-hand. He had cooked a stock pot with smoked sausage and some *porc* Genier had given them — God knows where he'd got it. It was bubbling away in the range, and the aroma filled the kitchen. He had lit the fire, and put the children to bed in their new room, reading to them from the only storybook they had.

She perched against the sink, a bird about to take flight. Pierre remembered those other days, sitting hour after hour in the gloom, Thomas mending his nets, the same net, hopelessly.

'You must miss your grandfather,' he said, breaking the silence.

She turned her back and peered through the window, above the big, square sink.

'It's so lovely here,' she said quietly. She turned to look at him and took a deep shuddering breath.

'What happened to Jacques, Papi's friend? Did he die?'

'I think he was shot, not long after. When the Germans took reprisals.'

'I always thought it was my fault. What happened to my grandfather, bringing you here. All my fault. Because I wanted to do something, you see. Something for the war. I was so angry, after my parents were killed. I wanted to get away too. If I were honest, I wanted to get away. I was never content.'

'Don't blame yourself.'

'Often, in that place, I thought about the farm, about *Le Tamaris*. It seemed like a paradise. I clung onto it in my mind when ... things ... happened. I could never understand, then, why I'd tried to run away from here. There, in that place, it seemed a perfect dream. But now ... now I'm here, I can't even sleep in my own bed, in my own room. I am too afraid — too afraid of being enclosed. Trapped!'

She stopped.

'Forgive me! Now, you see ... this is terrible of me, just for now I want to be alone with the children, raise them myself. I don't want to be owned by anyone. We've been through so much, and I feel terrible that the burden is on you. And you could never understand.'

'I could try, if you would tell me.'

'I will never talk about it.'

She stretched out her arm to him, and for the first time let her sleeve fall back. He saw the number tattooed there. She looked down.

'That was from Auschwitz,' she said quietly. 'Before I was moved to Ravensbrück. You cannot see what was done to me in Ravensbrück. They did experiments on us. Of course, they never sterilised the instruments. What did they care? Now I can never have more children. You would not want me. You have done your duty. Finding the children was a miracle. I will never forget it. But I can't be owned. The Russian tried to own me after the war, before the gulag. He was kind enough, but he thought I was his. No one will ever own me again. I have my children. That's enough.'

'Would it be better if I went away for a while? Maybe then you could have some peace, think things through. I could move into the town, if that would help.' It was hard to say.

She looked at him, considering. 'You mean ... you could still come here sometimes?'

'Yes. I could come sometimes.'

'In any case, we have the children now. They would miss you. They would need to see you.'

She took a gulp of wine.

'Oh, Pierre! You had done such a good job. They were settled. Now I'm making them afraid again, with my fear. It's not how it should be.'

She turned and with that swift step, squatted down beside him, her white hands on the table. Pierre looked at her in that dim light from the window, and thought how much he loved her. He saw how she had aged — lines around her mouth, her eyes sad. Her beautiful red hair streaked with white. Suffering was marked across her face.

'I will always love you, Rebecca. You know that.'

It was difficult for him to say these things. He had always found it hard to talk about his feelings. 'I love the children. I've tried to make a home for us here. It was for you too — though I never really believed you would come home. But if you need me to go, I'll go.'

He was still seated at the long table, and she bent down with her long frame, wrapping her arms around his shoulders. Briefly, she laid her cheek against his. It was almost the first physical contact since her return, the first time she seemed tender towards him. They were together for a moment, in that dark kitchen, with all its memories.

'I'm so sorry, Pierre, I'm broken. I have nothing to give. Perhaps taking care of the children, the farm, by myself, will give me back something. Maybe I can be mended. Who knows?'

'I understand. But don't send me too far away. I would like to come and help you on the farm, see the children, do what I can. We don't have to be together. I'll never ask that.'

Pierre stood up from the table. He longed to hold her, was sick with longing for her.

'Come! Come and see the children,' she said. 'Come and say goodbye.'

She took his hand, and they went up the narrow stairs together, she leading him like a child.

He thought then that they had never made love there. In the woods, in the tree hollows, in the house of the Benedictine Friars (silently, guiltily), in his hard single bed in Suffolk, that magical first night in the cottage. All that, and then only goodbyes. Now, it seemed, they could never have that again. It felt like a last goodbye.

Quietly, Rebecca opened the door of the children's bedroom.

The beds were empty, covers flung back. The little door to the outside staircase was open. They had slipped out while they were talking or, God forbid, had been taken. Rebecca gave a dreadful scream.

'Marie, my baby! Aishe!' She hurled herself through the doorway, down the steep stone stairs which hugged the outside wall. Pierre followed her, his heart thudding. The familiar farmyard with its mud. Ducks and geese once more on the pond. Water rippling in the moonlight. They called, shouted, from side to side in a blind panic, ran into the hay barn. It was empty. Had they been taken? There were vagrants about all the time now in the countryside, wandering the lanes in desperation. Rebecca was screaming the children's names.

'Where's the dog? The dog has gone too!' Pierre tried to calm her. 'Wherever he is, they will be! I'll get the torch. Then we'll go down the track to the telephone at Genier's place. Call out the gendarmes. Don't worry. It's only half an hour since I checked them. They can't have got far.'

Rebecca was weeping uncontrollably.

'I should have been in the house. I should have looked after them!'

She ran across the yard to where he had built her little shelter, impatiently pushing aside the tamarisk which served as a curtain. 'I'll get my blanket to wrap them in, when we find them. Please, God, we'll find them!'

She stopped suddenly.

'Oh, God, Pierre!' Lit by a shaft of moonlight, the two children were asleep, their arms around each other, curled up on the wooden bed Pierre had made for Rebecca, Petsha beside them. They stirred and opened their eyes.

'Mama? Is that you?' Aishe said sleepily. 'We wanted to be with you. But you wouldn't come into the house. Marie and I were afraid you would go away again.'

Rebecca crawled into the shelter on her knees, holding out her arms, just as he had seen hens in the yard gather their chicks when danger threatened.

'I will be in the house now. I promise. I will be there beside you. I won't ever leave you. I will always be here. Always.'

Then they were holding each other, crying, and she was kissing their faces through her tears.

It was time for him to go.

39

For more than a year Pierre just existed, in exile from the farm, living in Sainte Croix. He earned his living by stacking fish boxes on the quay, doing odd jobs in the town. He went to the farm occasionally to see the children. As she regained her strength, Rebecca had been rebuilding the rest of the farm buildings — with help from Paul. She wouldn't let Pierre get involved. Though part of him understood this was something she needed to do, he felt cut off — from the farm, the animals, but most of all from the children and from her. Edward tried to persuade him to come to England, but he couldn't be far from them or what felt like his place. His ties went too deep.

Rebecca came to see him one evening in his lodgings over the café/restaurant. He was cooking dinner for himself. He had become quite a good cook in those months at *Le Tamaris*, caring for the children, and he couldn't afford to eat in the restaurant every night. When the bell rang, he thought it was Paul, who sometimes came to report how things were at the farm. When he saw her standing in the street, he was afraid.

He poured her a cup of strong coffee from the *cafetière* he always had on the go. She sat nursing it, not speaking. He offered to share his meal but she shook her head. There was something very quiet about her which unnerved him. What if he lost her and the children completely? He loved the farm, but that wasn't so important. He could begin again anywhere — however hard it would be to leave a place he loved.

'How are the children?' he asked at last. 'Is Marie still making progress on the piano? What about Aishe? How are her songs coming on?'

'The trouble is, Marie refuses to learn with anyone else but you. And she's being difficult at the moment.' She took a sip of coffee. 'She misses you. So does Aishe. Aishe's uncle came back and taught her more songs. She began to sing them but now she keeps asking to sing them to you. She says she won't sing them to anyone else. Every night when they go to bed, they ask me where you are.'

He listened with mixed feelings, glad that they missed him, sad they were unhappy.

She shook her head. 'I know you can never know what we have endured, and I can never talk about it. It will be a closed part of our lives, one we can never share. And I need you to understand, I never want to be owned by anyone again. But then nothing is ever perfect, is it? I suppose I have begun to understand how much you mean to the children, and ... maybe ... to me.' She took a deep breath. 'I've come to ask if you would come back to *Le Tamaris*. If you can bear it. If you can bear to be with me. No! Of course, you don't even have to be with me. I don't think I could be with anyone at the moment — but maybe, some time, things will get better. Who knows? Anyway, of course, it's not your fault. None of this is your fault.'

40

It was very early morning at the farm. They had finished all their tasks and Rebecca had been outside to cut fronds of tamarisk to weave into a bouquet, the pink flowers already beginning to open in the early spring. She laid them out carefully on the kitchen table, with blooms from the garden and some others, a gift from Genier's daughter Eloise, the florist in Château-le-Vigny. She had come yesterday with flowers from the family, and a good luck card. It was an important day for them all, for the village as much as for them. Since Genier's suicide, they had all become much closer.

They piled into the old car with the flowers and cases for an overnight stay in Paris. Somehow, they had to find room for Edward who was flying in this morning, with his new wife. He was 90 now, but still sprightly, and he wanted to be there for this important family occasion.

Pierre was glad they had splashed out on the luxury of a box — a one-off on this special evening. Aishe's Uncle Harman and his wife were there too. They hadn't seen him for a while, since the girls went away to study in America.

Rebecca looked wonderful in her blue dress. The pearls he had bought for her fortieth birthday glowed softly around her neck. She was still as beautiful as ever, her red hair, now almost white, piled on her head and fastened with a diamante pin, a stray curl escaping rebelliously down her neck. She still wouldn't marry him, scandalising their part of rural France, where attitudes changed slowly. She was a successful businesswoman — running a chain of fishmongers' shops and stalls across Normandy — relishing the fact that in their snobbish little world being a fishmonger was looked down upon, even if it made you rich. She was still the rebel she always was. It had kept her alive. Her imprisonment in the concentration camp, those months detained in the Eastern sector, had only deepened her rebellious nature. She had never spoken again about Ravensbrück, and only briefly about her time in the 'filtration camp' in eastern Russia. After the Russian officer abandoned her, she had been caught up in the flood of Russian prisoners-of-war Stalin condemned to the gulags. That's all Pierre knew. Most of that time would remain a mystery. Meanwhile, their girls were enough. They were both profoundly grateful for their survival, against all the odds.

The lights went down, and the orchestra began to play. An empty piano stood in the centre of the stage. Now, as the last notes of the violin died away, Marie walked into the spotlight, very pale, red-haired, graceful in black velvet, every inch her mother's daughter, and behind, Aishe in a green silk dress, long black hair tumbling over bare shoulders.

Marie sat at the piano and began to play, holding the audience in a breathless spell. Rebecca leaned forward on the balcony, her face alive with pride. Then Aishe began to sing, Marie accompanying her, songs from Brahms' *Zigeunerlieder*, and wild, gypsy pieces they composed together. Pierre remembered their beginnings in the old kitchen at *Le Tamaris*, Aishe dancing round on the flagstones, clapping her hands, Marie flushed at the piano, laughing. Every so often, Aishe would play her mother's *cimbalom*; her uncle's tuition almost unnecessary. From that first day she seemed to know how to play instinctively. He remembered those summers when they used to sit underneath the flowering tamarisk, surrounded by chickens, and Aishe would sing Romany songs to Marie, songs she had somehow miraculously absorbed from her mother in those first terrible years of life, songs which had never left her.

Songs too that her uncle and her Romany family had taught her on their visits to the farm.

This is the first time they had performed together in Paris since they studied at the Conservatoire, the first time Pierre and Rebecca had heard them in concert for several years, since they left for New York. Only Rebecca perhaps, sitting in the box beside him, fully understood the journey they had made. It was a closed world to him, however much Pierre struggled to understand.

The last song, composed by the two sisters, was a poignant poem of loss and reparation. Its strange, wild theme had already been a hit all over the world with concert audiences, striking a chord with those still recovering from war, a hymn to the Roma who had been killed by the Nazis and dedicated to Tsura, Aishe's mother. The girls had composed it together after the whole family had visited Saintes Maries de la Mer in the Camargue with Uncle Harman in May, for the annual Romany Festival in honour of their patron saint, Sainte Sara. For the first time Aishe was part of a celebration of and for her own people. It was an overwhelming and inspiring experience for both girls. Now Aishe accompanied the song on her mother's *cimbalom* while Marie played. Marie was spoken of as a new young pianist of great talent, her passion and technique praised by critics everywhere from Sydney to New York. She was still hesitant and shy, her speech uncertain, but music was her gateway into the living world.

The audience were on their feet, clapping enthusiastically. The girls came forward together, bowing over and over again, their faces flushed. Flowers were thrown at their feet from the audience. Rebecca had slipped from her seat and now she appeared onstage holding out the bouquet. Flowers from *Le Tamaris*, flowers from all those friends in their Normandy community who had supported the girls so generously with love; woven with tamarisk fronds from the trees on the farm, gathered that morning. The trees had become a symbol of sanctuary, of new beginnings, of healing, the first place, under their branches, they had felt safe in their young lives.

Hand-in-hand, Marie and Aishe journeyed together into a bright future. No longer victims, survivors.

Bibliography

Arbib, Robert S. Jnr. (1947) Here We Are Together: The Right Book Club

Calder, Angus (1971) The People's War: Panther

Churchill, Peter (1954) Of Their Own Choice: Hodder & Stoughton

Cowburn, Ben (1960) No Cloak, No Dagger: Jarrolds

De Beauvoir, Simone (1964) The Blood of Others: Penguin

Drifte, Collette (2011) Women in the Second World War: Pen & Sword Books Limited

Foot, M.R.D. (1966) S.O.E. in France: H.M. Stationery Office

Foot, M.R.D. (1976) Resistance: Eyre Methuen

Foot, M.R.D. (1978) Six Faces of Courage: Eyre Methuen

Fourcade, Marie-Madelaine (1973) Noah's Ark: Allen & Unwin

Hampshire, A. Cecil (1978) The Secret Navies: William Kimber

Hawes, Stephen & White, Roger (Editors) (1975) Resistance in Europe 1939-45: Allen Lane

Holden, Wendy (2015) Born Survivors: Sphere 2015

Humbert, Agnes (2008) Résistance Memoirs of Occupied France: Bloomsbury

Instone, Gordon (1971) Freedom the Spur: Pan

Johnson, Derek E. (1978) East Anglia at War 1939–45: Jarrolds

Keegan, John (1982) Six Armies in Normandy: Jonathan Cape

Le Chêne, Evelyn (1973) Watch For Me By Moonlight: Eyre Methuen

Masson, Madelaine (1975) Christine: Hamish Hamilton

Millar, George (1973) Maquis: Mayflower Books

Mitchison, Naomi (1985) Among You Taking Notes... The Wartime Diary of Naomi Mitchison: Oxford University Press

Nicholas, Elizabeth (1958) Death Be Not Proud: Cresset Press

Panther-Downes, Mollie (1972) London War Notes 1939–45: Longman

Perry, Colin (1974) Boy In The Blitz The 1940 Diary of Colin Perry: Corgi

Report by The Supreme Commander to the Combined Chiefs of Staff on the Operations in Europe of the Allied Expeditionary Force, 6 June 1944 to 8 May 1945 (1946): H. M. Stationery Office

Settle, Mary Lee (1966) All The Brave Promises: Heinemann Ltd

Tickell, Jerrard (1960) Moon Squadron: Hodder & Stoughton

Tickell, Jerrard (1973) Odette: Kaye & Ward

"Vercors" (1968) *Le Silence de La Mer*; Jean Bruller, *The Battle for Silence* (film, 1949): Collins

Verity, Hugh (1978) We Landed by Moonlight: Ian Allen

**TOP HAT
BOOKS**

Top Hat Books

Historical fiction that lives

We publish fiction that captures the contrasts, the achievements, the optimism and the radicalism of ordinary and extraordinary times across the world.

We're open to all time periods and we strive to go beyond the narrow, foggy slums of Victorian London. Where are the tales of the people of fifteenth century Australasia? The stories of eighth century India? The voices from Africa, Arabia, cities and forests, deserts and towns? Our books thrill, excite, delight and inspire.

The genres will be broad but clear. Whether we're publishing romance, thrillers, crime, or something else entirely, the unifying themes are timescale and enthusiasm. These books will be a celebration of the chaotic power of the human spirit in difficult times. The reader, when they finish, will snap the book closed with a satisfied smile.
If you have enjoyed this book, why not tell other readers by posting a review on your preferred book site.

Recent bestsellers from Tops Hat Books are:

Grendel's Mother
The Saga of the Wyrd-Wife
Susan Signe Morrison
Grendel's mother, a queen from Beowulf, threatens the fragile
political stability on this windswept land.
Paperback: 978-1-78535-009-2 ebook: 978-1-78535-010-8

Queen of Sparta
A Novel of Ancient Greece
T.S. Chaudhry
History has relegated her to the role of bystander, what if
Gorgo, Queen of Sparta, had played a central role in the Greek
resistance to the Persian invasion?
Paperback: 978-1-78279-750-0 ebook: 978-1-78279-749-4

Mercenary
R.J. Connor
Richard Longsword is a mercenary, but this time it's not for
money, this time it's for revenge...
Paperback: 978-1-78279-236-9 ebook: 978-1-78279-198-0

Black Tom
Terror on the Hudson
Ron Semple
A tale of sabotage, subterfuge and political shenanigans
in Jersey City in 1916; America is on the cusp of war and
the fate of the nation hinges on the decision of one young
policeman.
Paperback: 978-1-78535-110-5 ebook: 978-1-78535-111-2

Destiny Between Two Worlds
A Novel about Okinawa
Jacques L. Fuqua, Jr.
A fateful October 1944 morning offered no inkling that
the lives of thousands of Okinawans would be profoundly
changed—forever.
Paperback: 978-1-78279-892-7 ebook: 978-1-78279-893-4

Cowards
Trent Portigal
A family's life falls into turmoil when the parents' timid
political dissidence is discovered by their far more enterprising
children.
Paperback: 978-1-78535-070-2 ebook: 978-1-78535-071-9

Godwine Kingmaker
Part One of The Last Great Saxon Earls
Mercedes Rochelle
The life of Earl Godwine is one of the enduring enigmas of
English history. Who was this Godwine, first Earl of Wessex;
unscrupulous schemer or protector of the English? The answer
depends on whom you ask...
Paperback: 978-1-78279-801-9 ebook: 978-1-78279-800-2

The Last Stork Summer
Mary Brigid Surber
Eva, a young Polish child, battles to survive the designation of
"racially worthless" under Hitler's Germanization Program.
Paperback: 978-1-78279-934-4 ebook: 978-1-78279-935-1

Messiah Love
Music and Malice at a Time of Handel
Sheena Vernon
The tale of Harry Walsh's faltering steps on his journey to
success and happiness, performing in the playhouses of
Georgian London.
Paperback: 978-1-78279-768-5 ebook: 978-1-78279-761-6

A Terrible Unrest
Philip Duke
A young immigrant family must confront the horrors of the
Colorado Coalfield War to live the American Dream.
Paperback: 978-1-78279-437-0 ebook: 978-1-78279-436-3

Readers of ebooks can buy or view any of these bestsellers by
clicking on the live link in the title. Most titles are published
in paperback and as an ebook. Paperbacks are available in
traditional bookshops. Both print and ebook formats are
available online.

Find more titles and sign up to our readers' newsletter at
http://www.johnhuntpublishing.com/fiction

Follow us on Facebook at https://www.facebook.com/
JHPfiction and Twitter at https://twitter.com/JHPFiction